The Crown Prince

A Royal Christmas Romance

By Amber Burns

Published by Scarlet Lantern Publishing

Prologue

Meghan

We had plans, solid plans. All the way down to having prepaid for plane tickets and a condo through a website where people rented out their homes to vacationers. We had plans. We were going to spend a romantic Christmas together. Then James was going to propose, and we were going to have our happily ever after.

We had plans.

Then I came home one night early from work. I wanted to celebrate an unexpected bonus from my boss. I came home to find the man who was supposed to be the love of my life in bed with another woman. He was supposed to propose to me. We were supposed to live together happily ever after.

We had plans, and he threw them all away for one night with some faceless, nameless girl.

What was I going to do now? How could I let this happen? Where did I go wrong?

My friends insisted that I take a trip to recover from this recent ordeal. I'd been living with James for six months. Six wasted months. In total, two years of my life had gone to waste. I didn't even have an idea as to how long he'd been cheating on me. For all I knew, it could've been the entire time. I'd been sure to give him his eviction notice, the apartment was mine. I'd also been sure to take thorough pictures of where everything belonged. While I hadn't had the opportunity to yell and scream at him for his transgressions, I wanted to make sure I had all my p's and q's covered.

The pictures and eviction notice were done at the suggestion of my boss, Wilson Marks. Mr. Marks was a divorce attorney, and he knew how bitter exes could be, even when they were in the wrong. Even though James and I hadn't been engaged, sharing space with another person could lead to lost items. Mr. Marks also suggested I supervise James moving out, but I didn't have the nerve to. I felt too fragile to stay around him any longer. I didn't want to hear his voice, I didn't want to take any chance of caving and letting him stay.

I had the eviction notice emailed to James, and then I blocked his number. It was cowardly, but I had a hard time facing him again. I didn't want to hear his excuses or have him try to woo me back. I didn't want to be fooled twice. And if I didn't give him the opportunity, I couldn't be fooled again. So I had to get away.

1

Meghan

It took blood, sweat, and a river of tears to get me to Miami. It had been the plan, where our romantic getaway was going to be. I couldn't get a refund on the plane tickets, but I could get at least one shifted to a standby ticket for another day. Small victories. I used the deposit that I had made through the website to splurge on the priciest condo I could find on the beach. Plus at this point my options were slim; all the snowbirds went to Florida for Christmas.

It took my entire bonus to pay for this trip, but I was determined to make what was supposed to be romantic vacation a worthy getaway for my battered heart.

So, here I was just outside this gorgeous villa. The outside had the common stucco feature that most of the homes in the area boasted, but this one didn't look cookie cutter at all. It looked as if it had been plucked from a Spanish coastline and plopped right here for me. There was a set of large dark oak wooden doors that led into the villa, and as I approached, I couldn't help but be struck at the hand-carved palms that decorated the outside of it.

Gorgeous wasn't an adequate word. But I struggled to think of another one.

I could only imagine what the inside looked like if the front door looked like this. I dug through my purse to find the key that had been mailed to me. I was eager to investigate, and this was the first time I hadn't had James and his indiscretions clouding my thoughts. I unlocked the right door and opened it slowly, taking a moment to admire the polished wood one last time before I stepped in and closed it behind me. I turned to have my breath taken away almost immediately. A small foyer led into an open great room that was decorated sparingly with one large sea foam colored sofa and two coordinating chairs set in front of it. The colors were set off by the wood tones of the end tables that stood out on the white tiled floor.

Is that marble? I asked myself.

I looked underfoot for a moment as I tried to discern it, but I could only assume. The wall opposite to me was made up of windows, all of which appeared to be open. I could hear the waves crashing upon the beach that I could see just feet away. I could smell the salt air and feel the breeze wafting in. It was breathtaking.

Why are they open? It looks as if that would invite any vagrant in. Maybe the owner arrived before I did to prep it? That was kind of them.

I decided that I'd come back to this view after I explored the rest of the home. I was starting to feel the fatigue of the flight. It was a short plane ride from New York to here, but all the bustle of it still tired me out. I followed a small hallway that was split off of the main room by a beautiful display of tropical plants that I couldn't even begin to name. I found a bathroom that was decorated in the same classy beach theme in blues that went with what looked like a sandstone colored tile. The bathtub was massive, and I couldn't wait to curl up in it.

Is this the only bath or is it a guest bath? I would find out soon enough.

I left the door open so I could remember just where it was for when I needed it and went further down the hallway where I found a guest room that was larger than my own bedroom at home. The bed was a king, also larger than mine, and had a delicate canopy that hung from the ceiling. The bed itself called to me with a promise of comfort and sleep. I didn't imagine this was my room, not yet anyway. I knew from the listing that the house had three beds. I had tried to talk my girlfriends into joining me on this trip, but of course, they had other plans. Christmas was coming after all, and they wanted to be with their loved ones... their significant others, something I was now lacking. The thought made my stomach twist into a knot, and I pushed away from the doorway of the bedroom to continue my exploration.

I found another bedroom similar to the first, decorated in a slightly more masculine theme. There were more hardwoods that stood out on the white walls and no canopy. The bed was also a king and looking at it made me anxious to crash into the next bed I saw.

At the end of the hallway, I found what I assumed was the master bedroom. It was far larger than the other two, and it looked like it dwarfed my little living room back home. The bed was huge; it had carved banisters that held up gauzy curtains that shifted delicately in the wind. The opposite wall, much like in the great room was made up of windows that were open to let in the sound of the ocean.

I was captivated. I didn't even bother with the rest of the house, which I was sure there was more of. I was swept away by fatigue and the salt smell. I went to the bed like a zombie and collapsed onto it. It was both soft and offered necessary support. I relaxed into it, and without a second thought, I let it sweep me away into a nap.

2

Demetri

I'd been dozing in the hot tub… right, not the safest of ideas, I know, but I was comfortable. It was hard to not doze off after the night I'd had. My beauty rest, and chance at drowning, was interrupted by the obnoxiously loud opening of a door then its bang when it closed.

Is that the front door? Or am I still drunk and hearing things? I relaxed back in the bubbly warmth and chalked it up to the latter. *The hangover hasn't set in yet, so I must still be drunk.*

But, before I could doze off again I could hear every door open. That's the pity of a house that's near empty. Every noise seemed to echo as it bounced off every surface and set you on edge.

So, I figured, *someone has gotten in.* I was sure I locked the door when I got in this morning, but I guess there was a chance I didn't. I released a groan and stood, best investigate then.

I stepped out of the tub and onto the deck that surrounded it. *Bugger, forgot a bleeding towel.* I shook off like a wet dog and decided that was well enough when I got struck by a wave of nausea. If the noise was nothing, I'd take the opportunity to get a bloody mary to help ward off the persistent hangover. I wandered into the master bedroom, still dripping, but I didn't give a fuckall. I was halfway to the bath when I noticed a set of legs hanging off the bed.

Now, legs happened to be one of my favorite things about a woman. So, the towel I needed was forgotten, and I wandered closer to see what kind of beauty had found her way into my bed. The legs weren't tan like I usually saw in South Beach, but the pale pallor didn't throw me off in the least. They were shapely, and they went up to a pair of round hips that I wouldn't mind resting against. The girl wasn't wearing short shorts, which was a pity, but I was still able to see a healthy length of thigh. I bit a lip and decided to check out the rest of the view. She wore a simple t-shirt that hampered the view of her torso save the fact that it was a v neck and I was least treated to a glimpse of cleavage. It went up to a heart-shaped face with bow lips... that I wouldn't mind seeing wrapped around my cock.

The only shame here was that she came to my bed and then nodded off. I wasn't sure if my drunken self had called in a little surprise the night before, but I wasn't going to pass up the chance to wake up sleeping beauty with a kiss. I climbed onto the bed beside her and growled a low, "Good morning, beautiful," before I went to wake her with said kiss.

That's when everything seemed to go downhill.

Bright blue eyes opened and went wide, and then her hand connected with my face with a force that damn near knocked the remaining bit of drunkenness right from my head. I didn't know a girl could slap you sober.

"Who the hell are you?" she shrieked as she crab walked up to the headboard so fast that I had to blink to make sure I saw that right. My vision was a bit blurred considering how hard she hit me.

I sat up at the end of the bed, rubbing my aching cheek. "Deme," I grunted as I rubbed my face.

"No need to hit, love. It's too early for that kind of thing."

"Deme," she still sounded hysterical when she echoed it.

"Aye aye," I stood and started for the bathroom. "I don't know what I was thinkin' when I called you up, pet. But if you're going to be violent like that this early, then you can see yourself out."

Now I needed something for the headache that was forming. It looked like the bloody mary I had promised myself was going to have to wait.

"Where are your clothes?" Was the next shriek that followed me.

Bloody hell. I liked screamers and the like, but right now it was too much.

"I was in the tub," I found my way to the medicine cabinet in the bath and searched out a Tylenol to help cure my pounding head. "Don't act like you've never seen a kuk before. The whole innocent thing is a turn off on a call girl," I hated to be blunt because I knew I didn't have the patience for it. Especially after that slap.

"What the hell," she shouted like I was the criminal here. "Are you doing here?"

What the hell kind of question was that? I walked back out of the bathroom to look at her like she had gone mad because obviously she had.

"I live here, pet," I folded my arms over my bare chest, and I looked at her with a new set of eyes. She definitely didn't look like my usual type of girl. "Who the hell are you?"

"Live here?" she echoed as she covered her eyes with her hand, as if she couldn't take looking at me anymore. Her face had taken on a lovely shade of red though.

Fuck that. I was a sight to behold, and I knew it. These abs and thighs were something that every girl, paid or no, had their fun licking up. And my cock was not something to hide your eyes from. I felt insulted.

"The contract said I was supposed to get this house to myself," she blurted out then looked away from me all together before she went to dig in a little off-brand bag. She came up with a phone, and with a little work, she pulled up a screen that I wasn't going to be able to read from where I was. "I'm supposed to have this place until the third!" she squeaked out.

I came forward to get a better look, grunting and she got skittish. "Fuck off, babe, I only bite when asked."

I plucked her phone from her grasp to get a better look at what she was talking about. On the cracked screen was an email from the company that occasionally rented out the villa. It was a copy of a lease agreement, and sure enough, the dates were there for today, the twentieth of December until the third of January.

"Bugger all," I grunted as I handed her phone back to her. "Wait a fix, pet." I went to my bag that I had carelessly tossed into the closet.

"Please tell me you're getting clothes on," I heard grumbled from behind me.

Her words gave me the temptation to kick open the door and give her a show of me bending over as I dug through my shit, but I refrained. I found my phone, something I had turned off a week ago when mother's persistent ringing wouldn't stop. When I powered it on, I noticed a dozen texts from her and voicemails. Bugger.

The best route I could think to take right now was avoidance. I didn't want to deal with the pressure they were putting on me. I was only twenty-eight, and I felt like they were trying to smother me with responsibility. If they were so keen on me stepping up in the line to rule, they could come get me out here. I'd been in Florida for nearly a month, basically since the last spat we had about "the line of succession". I decided to keep ignoring it all.

I pulled out a pair of boxers, gave them a sniff, and figured they were clean enough for my unexpected guest. I slipped them on and walked out as if that would make the situation better.

"This is a mistake," I said to the girl. She still gave me a wide-eyed look as if I were still in the buff. "Let me call someone, and we can get it settled out so you can be on your way." I focused back on my phone as I queued up the finance guy that worked for father. He was the royal treasurer, or whatever. I waited for the call to connect, time differences and all that.

"Hullo?" a voice answered, it sounded tired. I figured I might have interrupted a nap. "Demetri?"

'Aye," I sang into the phone. "Charlie! It's Charlie, right?" I didn't wait for him to answer. "I am at the house on Amelia Island in the states. I've been here for about a month, and some broad has come to crash with a rental agreement. What's up with that?"

"It's Grant, actually," he grunted after I finished speaking. "The last word I had heard you were going to the cabin in Aspen. Had I known that you were in Miami, I would have pulled the house from its rental rotation."

"Yea, well," I only half listened. "I'm here now, and there's a woman here insisting that she rented the place. Do somethin'." As much as I'd enjoy female company, I wasn't into the idea of having some that were slapping something other than my ass.

I heard him groan and I didn't resist rolling my eyes, after all, he couldn't see me. "Offer her a full refund," he gave me as a solution. "See if she'll take it. I'm sure there's probably nothing else available on South Beach given the time of year."

I grimaced because he was probably right, I hazarded a look over a shoulder and found the girl seated on the end of the bed, pointedly not looking at me. That was a disappointing thing.

"Well, do that," I barked. I didn't care whether or not she could find another place. That wasn't my problem.

"You will have to use your funds and account to refund her," he said with a yawn he didn't bother to hide.

"Will I be getting reimbursed?" I needed to know since I lived off of an allowance of sorts. It was a generous allowance, given that I was the only son.

"Not immediately, you have to understand. There is the family Christmas gathering that you have opted out of participating in," he sounded as if he was enjoying what he was saying. "But I will be sure to reimburse you the moment you return home."

Fuck all.

"You're not a help," I growled into the phone and ended the call.

How much money do I have in my account? I quickly went to the app to check on it. My phone indicated that I had what equated to about fifteen grand in dollars in my account. Not a lot, but plenty to last me the remaining bit of the year... if I was frugal. *How much was the tab for this place?* I went to the girl and snapped a finger at her, "Let me see the contract."

I watched her roll her eyes as she handed me her phone. I grimaced at the cracks in the screen and scrolled down to the bottom of the email to see the total amount she was spending on this place. I nearly dropped her phone. If I refunded her, then the bit I had in the bank would be cut in half. I wasn't willing to give up that much money. That would make things boring and I'd have to go home sooner than I wanted.

How do I handle this? I asked myself as I eyed her and tried to figure out a plan. Her expression was what they called 'Resting Bitch Face.' My mood was getting worse by the second, but then I noticed her gaze flicker downward. I couldn't keep from grinning as I turned to sit beside her.

"How about we change plans, love?" I put an arm around her shoulders and drew her close. "How about instead of me refunding you, you stay and keep me company?" I leaned down closer to her, dropping my phone back on the bed behind me and hers in her lap. "That way you don't have to fight for another place to stay," I tipped her face up closer so I could see her clearly.

There was a sprinkling of freckles across the bridge of her nose. The fact that I could see them made me realize that she was barefaced. Not a stitch of makeup on. And she still managed to be this appealing? I was so dumbstruck by it that I let her pull away from me and watched her get up.

"If you own this place then you can leave," she challenged. "And let me have the place to myself."

I could go to Colorado, that was still an option, and then I wouldn't get stuck sharing a place with some nameless broad. But the more I looked at her, the more of a hassle I could see it would be to get there. The skies would be busy and flagging a private flight is costly. Staying in Miami with this woman would just be something I would have to endure.

"I'll feed you," I offered. She didn't look like a high bred woman. She most definitely wasn't famous. I was willing to bet this cost place her a pretty penny. "I'll keep the kitchen stocked with food and wine," I gave her my best come hither look. "And we'll call it even."

She looked like she was going to cave. "I get the master bedroom," she retorted.

Negotiations! This would be fun.

"You sure?" I looked back at the tangled sheets. "I don't do laundry, pet, and I don't like to sleep alone."

Just as predicted her face scrunched up in distaste. "I don't want to see you walking around naked," she all but growled.

"And why not? I bust my ass to look this good," I flexed a bicep for her. "I'm fuckin' eye candy."

"Wear clothes," she demanded back at me, though her blush made her face go a pretty shade of pink.

"Fine, fine," I waved her off. "I'll wear clothes, but," I raised my hand. "I will be freeballing… and in the hot tub, I go buff. Don't like it, don't get in the tub."

She clenched her phone in her hand, giving me a good idea how those cracks got on her screen. "Fine," she gritted out before going to fetch her suitcase. I took my time in enjoying the view when she added: "If you're going to have company, for the love of God, please keep it to the bedroom."

With that last bit of torture settled, she carried herself out of my room, I assume to stake a claim on one of the other two bedrooms. I released a breath I didn't realize I'd been holding. I was never really concerned about saving a buck, I never needed to. But if I had to wait to get my allowance until after the holidays, then I wasn't about to cough up half of what I had now just to refund someone.

I can make this work. I decided. *She might seem prudish now, but I bet I can win her over. Besides! I only have two weeks to deal with her. Maybe I could even run her off if she gets to be too much of a downer.*

3

Meghan

I fled to the bedroom at the opposite end of the hallway, as far away from that man as I could get. I immediately dialed my office, most people had started their holiday vacation like I did, but there were a few die-hards that liked to stick it out. It showed that they were true New Yorkers. I, on the other hand, was just a poor southern transplant. I worried for a minute that no one would answer, but after the third ring, I heard a not so friendly voice answer.

"Marks and Welsh attorneys at law," Jodie monotoned. Jodie was one of the receptionists and she wasn't entirely warm. Regardless of her shortcomings, she was one of my favorite coworkers.

"Jodie," I said in the way of a greeting. I started to speak again in the urgency of my situation, but she cut me off.

"Oh!" she cut in immediately and her tone changing immediately to something more chipper. "Meghie, thanks for calling to let us know you got in. We were worried, you know how that is," she paused to take a breath. "Was your flight good? How's that overpriced house you paid for? Does it seem worth using all of your bonus pay on it?"

"There's a man here, and he won't leave," I belted out before she could ask more questions. I sat down on the bed and immediately covered my face, the vision of his nudity seemed to be burned into my mind's eye. He didn't seem to have any shame at all, walking around as if it were no big deal that he was proud of himself.

It was bad enough that he *was* beautiful.

"What?" My friend cut through the vision of the naked man.

"There's a man here, and he won't leave," I repeated.

"There are squatters?" Her tone sounded disbelieving. "Did you get scammed?"

"He says he's the owner," I filled in. "I-I don't think he's a squatter," not looking the way he did. His accent was one I couldn't place either. He was definitely not American. I doubted he was poor either. "I wanted to talk to Mister Marks. I want him to look at this agreement and see if what he's doing is legal. This guy doesn't want to leave. Instead, he wants to stay here in the house with me."

"That doesn't sound safe. Does he look dangerous or crazy?"

"Not really," though honestly, I tried not to look too hard at him. The entire time I'd been in the bedroom with him, he'd done nothing but strut and pose. It was like he expected me to fling myself at him.

"Email me a copy, and I'll forward it to Wilson. However, he's been in and out of the office a lot so it may be a few days before he can get to it," she paused for a moment and I heard a concerned sigh before she continued, "do you have mace or a Taser or anything like that?"

"I don't," I pinched the bridge of my nose. "They wouldn't have let me bring all that on the plane. Just get Mister Marks to look at it and see if what he's doing is legal or anything like that. If not I want to be able to get him to leave or at least get a discount considering how much I paid for this place."

"Consider me on it, sweetie, stay safe!"

She hung up on me after that and I knew she would do just as she said. Anything to get her away from the reception desk.

I pulled up my email and forward the information I had from the website to the reception email. Then I sighed in defeat. I didn't have a lot of options outside of this. If he offered to refund me the amount I paid, that'd be all well and good, but the likelihood of me finding another house, hotel, or motel the week before Christmas was slim. It would mean my only options were to stay or see if I could catch a flight back to New York.

I wasn't ready to go home. I'd have to face James. I doubt he'd have moved out by now.

Maybe Deme wasn't that bad. Maybe he could walk around the house with clothes on. Maybe I could live in a slightly less grand room for the two weeks I was on vacation.

I glanced around the room I had retreated to. It wasn't as big as the master bedroom, but it was nicer than any hotel room I'd stayed in. I remembered the tub I'd seen in the bathroom, and the aches I felt from the flight here seemed to intensify. The bathtub seemed like the best of solutions.

I can be careful around this guy, I told myself. *There are locks on the doors. I can do this.*

I dug through my suitcase until I found my toiletries. I pulled out the tattered robe I had blindly packed in my distressed state. I was going to make the best of this.

I made it out into the hallway without running into Deme again. After I found the guest bathroom again, I started to relax. Just the sight of that massive tub had all my stress just melt away. I turned on the water and watched it fill. The room was larger than the average bath, twice the size of the one I had at home. I put my bag of toiletries on the counter of the large sink. There was only one, but it seemed like it was large enough to accommodate more makeup than I owned. My curiosity got me snooping. I opened up the cabinet under the sink and expected to find cleaning supplies. At least a plunger. Instead, I saw a row of bottles with labels that I couldn't read. I picked one up and tried to decipher the language. Each seemed different. I opened the one I held in my hand and carefully sniffed it.

It smelled like delicate lavender and something else I couldn't place. It was almost sweet. I carefully fished a finger into it and found it to be soap. Well. If I was expected to share my vacation with another person, I would definitely be taking liberties with everything I found.

I was surprised by how relaxing it made my bath. I soaked in the sudsy water after I'd finished washing up and just let the warmth sap the stress from me. I might have dozed off, it wouldn't be the first time I'd done that.

I didn't have a clue how long I'd been in or asleep until I felt the chill in the water when a noise roused me. I grimaced and opened my eyes to the glare of the lights over the sink.

"Oh," a male voice purred. "Sorry, love. I was just going to order up some lunch. I didn't want to be a prick, so I came to ask what you wanted."

That voice cut through the drowsiness like a knife. I sat up quickly and struggled to wrangle both my breasts together so I could cover myself, "What the hell are you doing?" I couldn't help but stare at this man and his audacity to waltz right in here.

"I came to ask what you wanted for lunch," he said it slowly, taking his time to enunciate each word as if I were the one from a foreign country. He had a damn accent that made it quite obvious he wasn't American. But at least he was dressed, even though I wasn't. He had a pair of sweats on that hung low on his hips, bringing attention to the pronounce v that seemed to form on muscular men. I only saw it because, of course, he wouldn't be wearing a shirt.

"In this country, we knock before we enter a room," I barked at him. "Get out," I was fighting to stay curled up so he couldn't see anything.

"I knocked," his full bottom lip came out in a pout, and he made no move to leave. "The door wasn't locked," he waved back at it. "And I made the point to look for you, love. But you didn't answer… I don't even know your name."

He looked at me expectantly. I sighed; at least he was connecting eyes with me instead of trying to get a look at me. Considering the eye full he'd given me before, that was something I guess I'd appreciate.

"Meghan," I gritted out, repressing the want to choke him. "I'll tell you what I want for lunch as soon as you get out and let me get dressed." I watched that pout come out again, and he wandered out of the bathroom like I offended him.

My decision to stay was already looking to be a mistake, and I'd only been here for a few hours.

4

Demetri

I should not have done that. I should not have done that!

Seeing Meghan curled up nude in the bath was something I should not have seen!

I walked into the living room trying to rub that vision out of my eyes. Instead, it danced around my head and sent blood rushing south. My prick at half-mast was just what she'd want to see too. I adjusted and went to the kitchen, for no other reason than to have the bar to hide the fact that I was more than a little happy about seeing all of her. It was a pity she didn't seem to enjoy the view I'd given her earlier. While I waited for her to get dressed, I got distracted by looking down at myself, flexing and trying to see what wasn't to like. I even went as far to give my cock a good hard look. It didn't have any odd marks, looked straight, and as far as I was concerned it looked better than any bit of meat she might see elsewhere.

What wasn't to like here? Maybe I came off too strong? I did assume she was a call girl. Maybe that was it. I grimaced.

"Bugger," I whispered to myself. "That wrecked any chance of getting a piece of that tonight."

Maybe I could wine and dine her tonight and get some fun later. It sounded like work, but after seeing those bare curves, I figured it would be a crying shame to not hit that at least once while she was here. Twice if I could manage it.

I was distracted by the prospect of things I could do to Meghan, and I didn't hear her approach until she cleared her throat. She was wearing a pair of white shorts that put the full length of her legs on display and a crew neck shirt that didn't offer me anything to work with aside from the covered curves of her breasts.

"What about lunch?" she asked and watched me expectantly; like I was going to cook something. She didn't know I was useless in the kitchen.

"What would you like?" I pulled out my cell phone out. "I'll call the chef to come make it for us. At most, it'll take an hour. But he's on call and usually quick."

"Is there food in the house?" She didn't wait for my answer, and came around the island to the refrigerator. I watched her inspect the contents with a frown. "Do you have bread? We could make sandwiches for lunch instead of upsetting someone to make them for us."

"It's what they're paid to do," I said without a thought.

I didn't miss her rolling her eyes, and I watched her poke around until she found a loaf of bread in the box next to the fridge. She tested it with a squeeze then went about pulling out cold cuts and other fixings. I wandered around to sit on one of the barstools so I could watch her create magic. She put together a sandwich that made my stomach clench in hunger. So, of course, after she sliced it diagonally and turned her back I couldn't keep from reaching forward to snag a triangle.

I bit into it and couldn't help the groan that escaped. She made this right in front of me, I didn't see her cast any sort of magic spell while she did it. "Tell me you work in a deli?"

When she turned back and saw my theft she frowned at me, "No. It's not that hard to make a sandwich."

I hummed as I continue to eat the half of sandwich I had stolen. "It's not, but if you make me another one I'll consider giving you the master suite. Actually," I swallowed the mouthful and waved away my first offer. "Make me lunch on the regular, and I'll give it up."

She shoved the rest of the sandwich towards me and went about making one for herself, "I don't know that I want to share a space with you."

I put a hand to my chest, "You wound me."

"You don't seem to be able to respect privacy," she pinned me with a dark glower.

"Again," I put both of my hands up. "I knocked." And I did. I just didn't wait for an answer.

"It happens again," she made a point cut her sandwich just as she cut the first, though there was something a tad bit more aggressive about it.

Point taken. "I'll be a good boy," I promised. I watched her turn back to the fridge to pull out two bottles of water. When she handed me one I felt inexplicably touched. I took it and found it hard to look at her. "I'll behave," I reiterated my intentions.

"I'm not making you lunch again," that caught my attention, and I looked back up at her. "You can make your own sandwiches." She took her plate and looked like she was going to abandon me here in the kitchen.

"Oi," I patted the granite top to the island. "You don't get to escape just yet, love." I took a sip of my water, I'd sobered up quite a bit before I came into the bathroom and I was keen on having the company now. "Have lunch with me."

Meghan hesitated, looking as if all she wanted to do was escape. But, she came to sit beside me at the bar. She sat down and without any offering of conversation and started eating her lunch. Well, then. Given that there wasn't anything else for me to do but eat lunch, I went about finishing up. I made it through half of mine before the silence started to kill me. "You got friends meeting you up here?"

"No," she said after a beat. "This is my vacation."

"So, you're here by yourself?" I asked because it didn't make sense. "For Christmas? Why spend all this money to be here by yourself?" Isn't this the time of year that you spend with family?"

They always made a big to do about Christmas back home. It was a massive event that involved everyone at the city center, and it was something I'd recently made a point in missing, the pressure was starting to get to be too much. I didn't want to face my parents or my people for that matter.

I was so caught up in my own thoughts, the sinking feeling of the knowledge of all the people I was disappointing, that I didn't catch on to her silence. Until she made a noise that sounded suspiciously like a sob. Every man has at least one weakness; I myself have more than I care to name. The one that hits me hardest is the sight of a woman crying, I blame my older sister for that. While Meghan hadn't turned her teary eyes upon me yes, I could see her struggle to hold back the emotions.

"I had plans," her voice was a hint of just how heartbroken she was. "They fell through."

Was all that I was going to get? I ached for her, but I didn't pressure her for more. I got up and went to the pantry... though it was more of a wine closet than anything.

"Do you have a preference?" I asked as I motioned to the rows of glass bottles.

"What?" The word gasped out, and it was clear that she was still on the cusp of her need to wallow in pity.

"Do you have a preference for wine?" I didn't wait for an answer and picked up a merlot that looked to have a decent year to it. "Not deaf, love," I brought it back to the island and sat it down. "In the case of heartbreak, there's only one thing to do."

She looked at me like I'd lost my mind, but she was kind enough to not call me on it. "What's that?"

"You drink," I gestured to the wine bottle. "You drink to your broken heart and to the new beginning all this mess gives you." I waved a hand back at the wine closet, "We have plenty of spirits to sustain us for however much you need to drink away the memory of the prick that broke your heart. And plenty more to celebrate you being single again." I put both my hands on the bar, feeling a need to make her feel better. The way I figured it, we'd be sharing a space for the next few weeks so I might as well make an effort to make amends for the shortcomings of my gender. "So, the question is do you have a preference?"

I saw a hint of a smile, "What goes well with sandwiches?"

5

Meghan

I let this strange man get me drunk. It was a horrible idea. I felt raw still from everything; the fact that I was still tired from the trip down here left me feeling vulnerable. That's what I was telling myself when I took the offered glass of wine he poured me. He'd didn't bother with social norms either, he filled it to the brim. After our lunch was finished, he coaxed me out onto the back porch, and we stretched out on matching chaise lounge. The wicker looked real and the cushions I sat on felt like they might be made from memory foam. I got comfortable, and Deme didn't make any other attempts at being inappropriate. He just sat beside me and filled my glass every time it got empty. I'd lost track of time, but I knew I was more than a little drunk when he started talking.

"So tell me," he hiccuped. "How'd you get out here by yourself? What ass in his right mind would let go of you?" His accent made the words garbled. How was I able to understand him sober?

I hadn't wanted to talk about what happened with James, I didn't want to get personal with a stranger. But the more wine Deme poured into my glass, the less I cared about him being a stranger. What harm could come from telling him what had happened? I gave him a glare as I considered him; he was draped across his chaise lounge and looked as if he had been placed there by a modeling team that was striving to sell overpriced lawn furniture by putting a handsome half-dressed man on it. What was the point in fighting it? I'd already told my sob stories to the ladies I worked with a dozen times. It's what made them encourage this getaway.

"I'd been in a relationship with a man for two years. We had moved in with one another a little over six months ago," I set the glass of wine down on the little table that was between us. "I caught him with another woman just after Thanksgiving."

Deme hissed lowly, and I watched him throw back what was in his glass with an ease I didn't think I could manage the half glass I had left. "That's rough. Why spend all this money though? Just to sit in a house by yourself?"

"I thought..." I looked away out at the beach. The waves lapped at the shore as if they were calling me out to come into the water. "I thought if I got away from it all, got away from him, I could get my head on straight, and I wouldn't feel like he gutted me."

"Oh," the lounging shirtless man next to me whispered like he was talking to himself. "I can't claim to know the feeling. But you have my sympathies. I'd offer to rough him up if I saw him. Does that make it better?"

I laughed to the point I snorted. The vision of him punching James' lights out was something I shouldn't have found funny, but here I was laughing obnoxiously.

"What? Is he a big guy or something?" he snorted dismissively, "I'm quick. I can knock a guy flat."

"Thanks," I rubbed my eyes, tears had started to trickle down, and I couldn't place what had started them. I sniffled and fought my way to my feet. "I'm going to lie down."

I wavered on my feet but managed to turn back towards the bank of open windows. I made it a step before I started to stumble. I flailed and saw the glorious face plant I was about to make before a strong hand caught me under my arm. I looked, and Deme was kneeling on the lounge I'd been on. He looked a whole lot steadier than I felt.

He eased me to my feet and got off the lounge to stand beside me. "Okay?" he asked. His hand was still where he snagged me while the other came to my opposite shoulder. "I didn't mean to get you sodden." He was so close now, and for some reason, the tenor of his voice had lowered. I almost felt it; it was like a hum against my stomach.

I tried to keep my cool, but given how I'd been so far today, I didn't think it was a feat I could achieve. But it was the first time I really noticed just how attractive he was. His tanned skin suggested that he had spent a generous amount of time out in the sun. He had a sprinkling of fuzz across his chest, and the hair on his face was telling.

"Why are you here?" I asked, somehow suddenly breathless.

"Didn't want you to hurt yourself, love," he was so close. His dark eyes were narrowed to slits, and for a second I thought he might lean down to kiss me.

That charged me in a way I wasn't prepared for. I didn't want a stranger putting the moves on me, especially when everything was fogged up from too much wine. I pulled away from him.

"I'm okay," I still sounded breathless. "I need to lie down," I started back into the house and used what I could get a hand on to keep myself steady. I was just glad he didn't hold on or insist that he walk me to my door.

I was almost in the hallway when I heard him call to me, "What about dinner? Don't go to bed snockered on an empty stomach." He sounded concerned, and it was an effort to not turn back to look at him. "You'll wake up sick."

This must have been a test. I reasoned with myself. *I'm being tested, there is no way I'd naturally run into someone so attractive at random like this.*

"Surprise me, just... just let me lay down," I managed the rest of the way to my claimed room before I crashed onto the bed. I tried to clear my mind of Deme; because I knew that if that concern was real, then there was no chance I was going to be able to resist that.

6

Demetri

I kept my word and respected Meghan's privacy. I took willpower, but I managed to refrain from going to check on her. I knew I needed to clear my head from all the wine, so I dozed out on the back patio like I had before she walked in the door. The plans I had for the night seemed to go out the door, even if they weren't anything I had set in stone. It seemed like a better idea to keep my temporary roomie company.

After what must have been a couple hours, I woke to my stomach cramping in revolt. I knew food was in order and fished my cell from my pocket to call Chef Maurice. He could whip something up before Meghan woke up and I could surprise her with dinner. As the phone rang, I realized that I didn't know what Meghan liked and thought I perhaps it would be a good idea to keep the meal more American cuisine. I also didn't know if she had allergies or intolerances so I figured it would be best to keep things simple. Once Maurice answered I filled him in on the circumstances. In short order, he arrived to begin cooking.

"You have a woman here?" Maurice asked as he readied his ingredients.

The way he asked put me on edge. "She rented the villa," I answered directly. "There was a mixup, and it didn't get canceled. I am being a polite host. Don't assume that it's more than that."

"I didn't assume anything," he went to the kitchen to start prepping whatever it was that he had planned. "Her Majesty has called upon me since you first arrived. It's best that you keep her informed, so no one else assumes anything."

I grimaced and pinched the bridge of my nose. I'm sure mother would be on the next jet here if she thought I was holding up with a girl. They were so desperate to see me settled that I wouldn't put it past her assuming I was serious with the first woman she saw me with. Even if the woman was both common and a foreigner. I, however, wasn't keen on the idea of getting married. I wasn't keen on the idea of ruling a country either.

I had realized I needed to escape after I finished my education at Oxford years ago. Father was grooming me to be a well-educated and level-headed when it came to stepping into his polished shoes. He often had me sit in on conferences of his advisers and listen to the problems our country faced. Most things seemed to be of an internal nature, mostly because we were small and often overlooked by our neighbors and allies. I didn't look forward to trying to solve the squabbling over budgeting and the like. Frankly, how the Monarchy had managed to survive this long was beyond me.

"Don't worry my mother over something that isn't there," I tossed over my shoulder wandered out of the kitchen, even though I wasn't sure that was the truth. I'd felt something while holding onto her for that split second, and I was still, still, struggling to digest it. I'd only touched the under part of her arm and her shoulder, and now I really wanted to see if the rest of her skin was as soft as the little bits I'd touched. That brief closeness seemed electrified, to the point that I was surprised I didn't see the sparks of it between us. Would it have shocked me to kiss her?

I've had too much to drink, I tried to write it off as just that. I'd spent the majority of my time here drunk and either here buried in a faceless woman or in a club surrounded by beautiful fake women. There was something about the heartbroken state of Meghan that seemed to pierce me in a way I wasn't prepared for. I couldn't imagine it had something to do with me wanting to fix anything. I definitely didn't have an edge or a clue as to how to do that. I'd broken plenty of hearts and was well versed on how to do so.

Maybe my best bet is to just leave her to drown in her pity? I could just let her stay here and keep on as I was before. That's what I should do. It's the smart thing to do. I reasoned.

Instead, I decided to go check on her as the first hints of something delicious started to ease into the air. I knocked on the door, putting a bit more force behind it than when I traipsed into the bathroom before. I didn't get an answer, as I suspected I wouldn't. I carefully opened the door, somewhat surprised that it wasn't locked.

Meghan was curled up on her side facing the door. She managed to look a whole lot smaller than I remembered her being. I refrained from going to her, though there was a temptation to do so. It was like a magnetic pull that I fought to resist. I couldn't keep my eyes from devouring every inch of her. Her face was slack, save for her brows pulled up tight like she was still trying to figure out what she had done wrong.

I didn't have the heart to tell her the only thing she'd done was love the wrong man. With a sigh, I turned and closed her door. I followed the smell of chef Maurice's cooking back into the kitchen, knowing I was eating alone tonight.

7

———————————

Meghan

I'd slept hard, I realized that when I felt all the aches that came with sleeping in one spot. Normally I tossed and turned. This time I didn't. I stretched out and spread out on the bed. At some point, I must've gotten cold because I was covered with a light blanket. I didn't remember getting up to get it.

My head felt fuzzy, and my mouth felt like it was a desert. I got up, and everything felt like it was in slow motion. Slowly, I made my way into the bathroom to the sink. The lights stayed off. I managed to drink from the faucet, cupping my hands together. I made a mess, soaking the front of my shirt and getting my hair wet but it seemed to help. The pounding hadn't started, but I could feel it on the horizon.

I was a little more even now, awake enough to move faster but cautious of the hangover that was standing at the ready, poised to attack. I got back into my bedroom and found my makeup bag. I'd need something to stave off the impending doom. Aspirin, Tylenol, Ibuprofen, at this point, I didn't care. Once I had a bottle in hand, I found my way back into the bathroom just as the ache in my head began. I shook a few little round pills into my palm and tried to swallow them dry. It made my mouth taste horrible. I didn't bother with trying to cup water to my mouth; I bent to slurp at it as it came from the faucet.

"You got that taken care of?" I didn't bother to see where he was at. His voice was quiet like he knew just how my head felt. "Need anything?"

"It just started," I managed between gulps of water. I hoped he'd understand and give me the space to be miserable. I put my head against the cool ceramic counter and breathed, trying to get everything under control.

I should have known this would happen. Why did I let him keep pouring wine down my throat? I'm such an idiot. My thoughts were interrupted when something hit the countertop, and I felt it rock inside my head.

"Drink this. It'll help. Breakfast is on the bar."

Confused, I straightened to see what he left me. Through a wave of dizziness and nausea, I saw a bottle of pale purple liquid. This was his remedy? Disgruntled, I picked it up and twisted off the lid. I'd be sure to not let him help with my break up again. I drank the offering he left greedily, grimacing at the taste. It was far too sweet, and the metallic aftertaste clung to my tongue in a way I was sure would have me diving for the toilet.

I was soon halfway through it, and nothing was coming back up. I gave the bottle a new look, glancing at the back label. The number of vitamins and minerals on it threw me, and I realized that Deme had brought me something for my hangover. I sat down on the seat of the toilet and made an effort to drink more of the foul tasting liquid. I started to feel better in fractions. Slowly, the pounding went to a dull ache, and the nausea became something a bit more bearable. Once I felt I was starting to regain control, I realized I had no clue how long I sat there in the bathroom.

"You alright now?" Deme's voice rang from the doorway. I hadn't heard him coming down the hall.

"What is this?" I gestured to the now empty bottle.

"I use it for my hangovers," he leaned against the doorframe as he spoke. He seemed quite content to just lounge around in the pair of shorts. "It helps with dehydration, I think. But it works quite well you'll find. Just give it a minute. Are you hungry?"

"No," it seemed like it would probably hurt to shake my head.

"Think you need another?"

"No," I croaked, but did feel like I needed more water, so I stood and went to the sink. I saw Deme disappear as I bent to drink from the faucet again.

"Get out of the sink," he had come back and set another bottle on the counter. "Let's get you back to bed and get you proper again." He helped me up and, with the bottle of water in hand, eased me back to the room I was staying in. "Just rest up, love," his voice was low as he got me back onto the bed.

"How are you not in the same shape?" I asked, a bit jealous.

"Drink enough on the regular, and you get used to it," he covered me with the blanket, and I felt the warm touch of his hand against my face. He brushed my hair back and didn't seem to mind that I probably looked like death warmed over.

"I don't enjoy feeling like this."

"Well, love," his voice was like honey, and I shouldn't have focused on him like I was. He was sitting close, and his hand seemed content to tangle in my sleep-mussed hair. "Plan B was to get you a Bloody Mary and get you snockered again. You want that?"

"I don't think it's a good idea to get drunk around you," the honesty of it sounded harsh, and I should have felt horrible for saying it. "Or again for that matter."

Surprisingly, he didn't look offended. "I'm not irresponsible like that. But you're right, it's never a good idea to drink around a stranger," he stood and adjusted his shorts. "Better off doing this sober anyway." He stood, and my still clouded mind didn't decipher the meaning behind his remark before he spoke again. "Sleep the sick off. I'll see if I can't find some biscuits to tide you over until you can have a proper meal."

I should have questioned it and him, but the thought of sleep was far more fetching. I dozed off, unable to fight it.

***

A sharp whistle brought me back to consciousness, and I didn't have a clue as to how long I'd been asleep. I sat up and, fortunately, I had slept off the horrible feeling from before. I noticed a few bottles and a packet of crackers on the bedside table. There was even a bottle of Tylenol. I rubbed at my eye as I reached for one of the waters. It felt like I had been in hibernation.

How long have I been asleep?

"Finally," Deme came into my bedroom without a concern. "Sleeping beauty has awoken!"

He was dressed, wearing the most clothes I had seen him in since I had gotten into the house. He had a pair of gray slacks that looked like they had been made for him. They hugged his hips and seemed to put emphasis on parts of him that I shouldn't be looking at. He also had a white undershirt on. It looked like he was getting ready to go somewhere. His short cropped hair was still damp but still a degree of messy that he could make seem attractive.

"Rise and shine, love," he went to my closet, I hadn't bothered to unpack, so I don't know what he was looking for until he came out with a dress stretched out in front of him. "You need to start getting ready for dinner and dancing."

"What?"

"Dinner and dancing," he came closer to the bed and held the dress out as if he could judge whether or not it would fit me. "Get up, go shower. Put your face on and let's go. You've slept enough."

"I don't want to go dancing," I argued that point, but I wasn't going to argue the idea of dinner. I had slept for what seemed like days, and it was catching up with me. My stomach clenched then rumbled.

"Love," he sat on the bed beside me, scooting in close enough to where I could smell his cologne. Its musk disoriented me, and I could only look at him confused. "Wallowing over the prick that shafted you isn't going to make things better. Fate," he set the dress aside on the other side of me. "Brought you to me and I'm going to do what I can to make you forget about him and your broken heart. You've been in bed long enough," he gave my hip a pat. "I promise to make the meal well worth it." He nodded towards the dress on the bed, "Give me a holler if it doesn't fit, and we'll find something else. But get beautiful, so the ole boy will know what he lost and regret it."

I wanted to argue. I didn't think it was a good idea to be charmed by this man that I barely knew. But instead, I nodded and Deme got up to leave me to get ready. I guess he had the right idea. It did seem like a massive waste of money to just spend my entire vacation wallowing in pity and wondering where I went wrong.

I was going to let go. It was time to let loose and forget James.

8

Demetri

It'd been nearly an hour since I'd given Meghan a pep talk and I found myself waiting in the living room for her. I wanted to be impatient, but the idea of inviting her out had been spur of the moment. I knew I could go out and get something that would be easy and not take an effort, but no. I couldn't get the leggy blonde that showed up at my villa out of my head. So I'd taken the extra step to see that she'd go out with me. I only hoped Nadine's dress fit her. Meghan had curves that my sister didn't, so there was a chance that I would probably be out a few hundred to get her the right dress to go out in. I pulled out my phone to check my balance, though I knew it wouldn't be too big of a deal. I could pinch some corners so that I didn't spend all my allowance at once.

Not going out last night had certainly saved me a few grand. I'd probably be spending that tonight, plus more by taking Meghan out with me. But if I could get her to unwind, it'd be worth it. The idea was to make her forget the bastard she left at home, and I might as well show her a good time or two while I had her with me.

I was cracking into a before-dinner brandy when I heard her. "The dress is tight," she heaved a breath. "But I guess if I don't eat too much or bend over I'll be able to manage the night." She didn't even look at me as she patted at her lower belly then her hips, "I couldn't fit in any of the heels that were in the closet. Will my flip flops be alright with this?"

I didn't really hear any of it. I was too caught up in just how she looked in the dress. On Nadine, it hung about respectably. On Meghan, it did nothing but accentuate every curve she had. The skirt length hit her mid-thigh, and I got to see every bit of leg. Even without heels. She had her hair loose around her face and curled around her shoulder. She was gorgeous.

This was a bad idea. I'd be competing with every man that laid eyes on her. If I didn't manage to appeal to her, then some other prick would get to that before me. I cleared my throat and tried to put myself back to rights, "Your old man is an idiot."

A flush went across her face and down her neck. Seeing her turn a pretty shade of pink made me wish I hadn't had the idea of taking her out.

We could just stay in. Save me some money and still manage to have some fun. I tried to reason with myself, though that was me being selfish. The chances of me getting anything out of tonight were slim. She didn't strike me as the type of girl to cut loose. I shook my head, trying to gather myself. I was thinking with the wrong head here, the idea was to help her feel better about herself.

"Thanks," she gave me a smile that touched me in a way that didn't concern my happy bits. "I didn't think I would look good in this because it was so tight. You said we were going dancing, too? That's probably a bad idea considering the way I look." She took a second to try to straighten the dress as if she could make it fit her better and make the material grow, so it wasn't so tight.

"There's a club I've kind of claimed as my own. It'll be fun," I shot back the tumbler of brandy I'd just poured. "Come on, the driver is waiting, and we can see what kind of trouble we can get into for the night."

She looked like she wanted to argue, her mouth opening then closing. But instead, she came to meet me and followed my lead.

I took her to one of my favorite restaurants in South Beach. I wined her and dined her in a way that I never bothered with other women. I couldn't get an understanding of the distinction, what the difference was between her and any other female I'd been with.

Was I actively trying to make an impression? If I hadn't managed to after our first meeting, I wasn't sure how this would make a difference. Was this an effort to get into her pants? Or was I actively just trying to show her a good time? Gut instinct told me it was the first, even if effort wasn't something I usually made. Never really needed to be honest. But, somewhere in me, I wanted it to be the latter.

Conversation over dinner was skittish at best. She looked confused at the start, like she hadn't expected a five-star joint. She spent the majority of the time perusing the menu and taking in the decor. It took an effort to pull her into a conversation, but as soon as I managed, I did my best to steer clear of any topic that may cause her to think of her reason for being in Miami alone for Christmas. Instead, I got to know her.

I didn't usually have the desire to do that, and she never questioned my motives. She seemed to willingly shed the insecurities she came with and opened up to me. It was mostly small talk, though I did my best to deflect any of her questions to me that got too personal. There was too much that I didn't want her to find out. But she didn't seem to mind opening up to me in the least. It was heartwarming.

By the time we got to the club, I felt less like a stranger. I felt like I had a better idea of who she was. Meghan wasn't the type to pick up a random man to take care of the memory of her ex, and the likelihood of me getting anything out of this was slim. But that didn't keep me from enjoying myself.

I made sure the bartender knew she was on my tab and then we found my usual spot. I could see the music humming through her; the thump of the bass seemed to give her an extra bounce even though all she had to drink was the red wine at dinner.

"You don't have to stick with me, love," I offered her a nod towards the dance floor where the majority of the clubs occupants were. "Go dance. If you need a drink, the bartender will take care of you."

"And you're staying here?" The look she gave me spoke of vulnerability, like she expected me to bail on her now that we were in a crowd.

"Yea," I tried to smooth any feathers by giving her my best smile.

She seemed to hesitate, I couldn't figure out why, but eventually decided to let the music pull her to the floor. I couldn't name what was being played. Honestly, it sounded like a rap song mashed with electronica. The beat was something I couldn't resist nodding my head as well, and when I found Meghan in the crowd, it looked like she couldn't resist it either.

She seemed fine with the idea of dancing by herself, her arms were over her head, and her hips rolled in time with the beat. I didn't concern myself with anything other than just watching and flagging down a waitress so that I could order a drink. I hadn't thought past having a night out and how I would feel with having my new friend along. I wasn't going to make it a mission to keep her entertained. Not when it was obvious that I wasn't going to get anything aside from the pleasure of her company.

I would just keep an eye on her. For safety's sake.

It didn't take long for a partner to find her. A man came up behind her and began to move in sync with her. I knew this was inevitable; she was a beautiful woman dancing alone. I was an idiot to let her go out there by herself. I realized that as soon as I saw this faceless man put his hands on her hips and it set me on edge. I scooted out of the booth and stood so I could keep a better eye on her but a set of hands wound around me, and I heard a voice in my ear, "Come cuddle with me, baby."

I had made something of a reputation for myself with the women that frequented this club. While none of them knew exactly who I was, they were well aware that I had money. I often bought drinks for girls that I shared my booth with, in exchange for company that was more than just friendly. Now though, I was watching Meghan distractedly, and I wasn't keen on the idea of letting a nameless girl rub on me. I stepped out of her embrace without much of a look back at her; I didn't care what she looked like.

"Sorry, love, not tonight."

I was too intent on what was happening on the dance floor. I watched with growing irritation as another man boldly put his hands on Meghan. Hands that drifted from her hips and up her sides with a purpose, I could feel my neck get hot, and the only course of action was the most obvious. My only problem was that I didn't have any claim to her. So I did the only thing I could, I wound my way down to the dance floor and shifted through the crowd to her.

I opted to stay in front of her so that both Meghan and the man behind her saw me. I fell into the beat, and since his hands had vacated her hips, mine found their way there. I made it a point to make it obvious I was dancing with the woman between us. I got a dark look that I readily returned to my competition. Meghan, on the other hand, gave me a smile I hadn't expected. Her hands fell on my shoulders, and it made it obvious to the prick behind her who she favored. I was rewarded with a sneer before he backed off. As soon as it was just her and me, I got lost. Whether it was the music or the just the feel of her against me… I couldn't say.

My plans for the night were immediately were dashed in favor of her rocking hips. Her eyes looked to be a darker shade of blue, a color I couldn't put a name to even after all the forced education I had gone through. I lost track of time, enjoying myself way too much. She rocked against me in a way that could be considered nothing but sexual. Did she feel it, too? There was no way I was the only one that felt this charge. If she got any closer, she would definitely be feeling the reaction I was having. I thought I would get away with the erection until I felt her pull away. I thought I was in for a slap until she pointedly mouthed "Bathroom" with a shrug.

It took me a minute to register what she wanted, but then I pointed her in the right direction. Once she left me, I found my way to the bar and tried to consider a plan of action from there. I could try to worm my way under her skirt, it was something I really wanted to do… especially having her pressed against me on the dance floor. Or, I could be the gentleman I was raised to be. It decided that it would probably be better to just show her a good night out, offer a friendship instead of a fling that couldn't amount to anything. It's something my mother and sister would expect me to do because there was nothing respectable about taking advantage of a lonely woman.

I decided, after a beer was placed in front of me, that I would do what was right. I wouldn't make an ass out of myself. Instead, I would just see to it that her vacation was something she would remember fondly and not something that would bring back memories of the man that caused her to be in Miami.

9

Meghan

Dancing, there was something about the movement and the beat of the music that just cleared everything away. At first, I was upset about having to go on the floor of a club I wasn't familiar with by myself, but once I got out there and got started I let it go. I hadn't paid any mind to anyone that took up the mantle to be my partner until Deme appeared. It seemed easy to fall into rhythm with him. I couldn't keep from putting my hands on him. He had his on my hips, so it seemed only natural. It was hard to ignore the pull he had over me as we danced together. The spark, the rush I felt seeing him that first time was there. I wasn't drunk, and there wasn't any buffer to keep me from feeling the attraction.

Or maybe I was just desperate to feel attractive. The looks he gave me since I first walked out in this borrowed dress only seemed to get more heated. He made me feel attractive with every look he gave me. I couldn't think of a recent time I'd gotten looks like this from James.

I lost myself, and I would have loved to just dance with him the entire night, but nature was persistent. I parted from him after getting directions and found the restroom. The break gave me time to gather my thoughts. I hadn't considered just what I could do with my vacation other than trying to figure out what I had done wrong. Then I remembered something one of my girlfriends had suggested: getting James out of my system with another man.

It seemed like a terrible idea. I wasn't someone that readily gave myself to another person. I wasn't appealed to the idea of getting personal with someone I didn't know. But, with all of this… I could use this to turn a new leaf. I could see the way he looked at me and I knew how it made me feel; it made my heart beat harder in my chest. If I quit repressing it, I knew the attraction was mutual. I could feel the undeniable want that I had for him. Why deny myself? One night stands were never my thing, but why not try it this one time? If there was a way to get the last bits of James that clung to me like a stubborn spider web, this was likely to be it.

I wandered out of the bathroom, finished with my business, and I didn't bother giving myself a once over in the mirror. It wasn't confidence, I just didn't want to face the mess dancing had created. I felt slick with sweat, and I was sure he was probably in the same boat.

Deme hadn't stayed out on the dance floor while I was gone. I went to the bar, my mouth felt like a desert, and I figured something with alcohol would help. I flagged down the bartender and waited for him to finish with the people he was busy with.

"I got you something," his voice cut through the noise of the club, and it struck me. I turned to see Deme behind me with a bottle of water in hand. "I figured," he gave me a smile that couldn't be described as anything, but sexy. "After our last adventure with wine, it would be better to offer you something easier to drink."

"Thank you," I took the offering and watched as he downed the rest of a glass of brown liquor.

"Did you want to get back to it?" His smile pulled me, and I realized then I was going to let go. I was going to do this. He gestured back towards the club's dance floor. "Let's get back out there then."

"Actually," I paused for a beat, I could see the question in his eyes, and I took the time to busy myself by taking a gulp of my water. "Could we go? It's been a day, and I'd like to get to bed."

"You sure?"

He looked surprised; maybe he was more of a night owl than I was. I nodded, hoping he would ask for more of a reason. I guess I was being a poor guest, especially since he was paying for the night. I should wait it out until he was ready to go. I watched him step away from me and pull out his phone. He looked like he was texting and I couldn't imagine who he would at this hour until he turned back to me to say, "Give it ten minutes, love. The driver is on his way."

We lingered by the bar, and I felt far too on edge to try to start any sort conversation. I was trying to work up the nerve to broach the subject of sex between us. But it kept dying on my lips, and for the first time since I started seeing James, I was nervous. It didn't stifle my want, the excitement that flared the life at the idea of being with another man. A very attractive man.

When he took my hand, a smile on his face, my heartbeat picked up. Did he know? He led the way to the door, gave the bouncer a salute and took us both out into the brisk night. It was at least sixty, and I was regretting not having brought a jacket. But like a gentleman, he stopped and shrugged out of the button down he was wearing, he dropped it on my shoulders as if he wasn't affected by the cool breeze in the white undershirt he sported now.

"I guess it's going to start looking like Christmas, eh?" He gave me a grin, "As close to Christmas as South Florida gets." He nodded towards the Town Car that had brought us out here, it was black and nondescript. He led the way to it, motioning me in when the driver opened the door for us.

I slid into the warm leather seats and scooted so Deme would have room. I didn't bother to offer his shirt back to him. I slid my arms into the sleeves that he had rolled up; they hit me about midway down my forearm. It wasn't a particularly thick shirt either, so it only offered a slight barrier the cool night. But I could smell his cologne and under it a musk that could only be him. I sat and just breathed it in. I didn't concentrate on it long because as soon as he got in beside me, he seemed to spread out. The man seemed to take up as much room as he possibly could.

Instead of taking advantage of it the situation and by getting closer to him. I made no moves to seduce him. He didn't make any moves on me either. It was a quiet ride, one that I was uncomfortable with, but he didn't seem to mind it at all.

I struggled to think of something to say before I just settled. "Sorry," I spared him a glance. "I know it's probably early for you."

"Don't worry yourself, love," he nudged me with his knee. "You had a good time, right?"

He'd been good company, and while I had been uncomfortable dancing on my own at first, he had come to join me. I didn't want to say how it made me feel, that I wanted him. We fell silent again until we pulled up to the house. The driver let Deme out first, but he turned to help me.

We walked to the door together, even down the hallway. I thought, with my heart hammering in my chest, he was going to take me to his room. Or maybe come into mine. But, all he did was wish me a good night with. I watched him go to the master bedroom, leaving me still wearing his shirt.

I had no idea where to go from here.

10

Demetri

I felt buzzed and while I hadn't found the fun I normally would on a night out, I still enjoyed the evening. I don't usually dance unless there was a pretty girl I wanted to convince to come home with me. But tonight wasn't about me, so I didn't bother with my usual game plan. It ended early, the clock barely nearing midnight, so I wasn't letting it cramp me up. I undressed down to my skivvies and opened up the doors to see the moon lighting up the sky and ocean. It was cool, though it would be colder back home than on any beach in this country. I had missed the first snow. I had missed the lighting of the tree and I would probably miss the bazaar in the square.

I was tempted to go pilfer myself another drink, something to shake the cold and get the thoughts of home out of my head. Instead, I let the sound of the waves on the beach distract me, along with the tang of the salt. I was in paradise. Christmas was just another day of the week. I shouldn't let it spoil my mood.

I heard a door behind me open, I'd left the lights off so I couldn't see who it was, but it could only be her. I turned, squinting to see her until she stepped out of the shadows of the room and stood just so in the moonlight. I couldn't help but take her in, the light making her look pale and otherworldly. It took me a minute to realize all she wore was the button down I'd lent her. Blood went south so quickly I got dizzy.

"Am I dreaming?" I breathed out.

Of course, she didn't answer. She didn't make it easy on me. She just looked at me as if she expected me to pick her up and ravish her on the spot. A tempting prospect, but here I was trying to figure out if I had drunk more than I thought. Had I passed out?

I watched, the hesitation was obvious. She looked unsure about her coming here, but she still stepped forward. "You took me out to help forget James," her voice was small, and she looked down at her feet. "Help me forget him," she said it like a plea.

It caught me off guard in a way I wasn't expecting, just like her sudden appearance. My heart thudded in my chest and my cock throbbed in response. Better sense should have told me this was a bad idea, but my brain lost control, and my cock decided to do the driving as it often did. I closed the short distance between us, and before she could voice any second thoughts, I leaned down to get my first taste of her. Our lips connected with a bit more force than was necessary, drawing a noise from her. It didn't sound like a protest.

Meghan didn't pull away or push me off. She just leaned forward into me, giving me complete control. I took my time enjoying the softness of her lips, the honey taste that could only be her lip gloss before I delved past them. I swept between her teeth and carefully coaxed her tongue into playing with mine. I tasted the honey flavor mixed with a bitterness that could've been from the wine we had a dinner. It didn't deter me from exploring every inch of her mouth.

Kissing her wouldn't be enough. Already after the first one, I wanted so much more.

I cupped her face and broke the kiss, tilting her head back so I could trace my way down to her jaw. The height difference wasn't going to have me be able to stand hunched down like this for long. But as I scraped my teeth against her jawline I saw her eyes flutter closed, the nervousness seemed to flow right out of her. She relaxed against me and seemed far more pliable. I slid a hand down to part the fabric she had conveniently left unbuttoned. God, she came in here with just my shirt on. It made me want her more. We couldn't do this standing up, and I couldn't lean down like this for much longer.

"Come on," I huffed out as I turned her around and started directing her to the bed. I was going to get impatient if I didn't watch myself. For some reason, I wanted this so much it was difficult to find restraint. I had only spied a look at her once, but that didn't explain the urgency I felt at needing to have her. I took a deep breath to try to calm down and carefully picked her up into my arms. She stiffened and looked unsure, but there was no effort in having to carry her. It was a clue that I might be a bit overly eager, more so than her. I was sure to set her down carefully so I could distract her with another kiss. I lingered too long for it, leaning down into her as I fit myself against her. She was smaller, but still managed to find a way to mold against me just right. It would take little maneuvering and clothing removal for me to slide right in.

But this wasn't a quick fuck; there'd be no sliding right in. I couldn't get away with being the only one having fun at this party. If this was going to happen more than once, then I needed to be smart.

I was charged with making her forget about her prick ex, I wasn't going to make a prick out of myself in the meantime. I couldn't be selfish like usual. I knew how to please a girl, and it was high time I went about doing that.

So, I dragged myself from her lips again. They were quite kissable, and I could entertain myself with the idea of having them wrapped around me another time. Only now without having to worry about developing any sort of aches or pains, I worked my way down to her jaw then to her neck. I worked my way down, opening the shirt as I went. Her breasts were perfect pert handfuls that I couldn't wait to cup and tease, not after the sight I had caught earlier in the day.

I saw the gooseflesh stipple across her skin as soon as my hand caressed her bare breast. It was a hint that she just might be as excited about this as I was. The nipple peaked with little stimulation, I couldn't contain the groan. I latched onto her breast and pressed my hips to her thighs just so she knew how turned on I was. I didn't want there to be any doubts as to how much I wanted this.

I traced a path from her breasts and I licked my way down her stomach. I shifted until I was between her thighs, putting a leg over each shoulder. I didn't hold back from the flushed skin beneath a neat little thatch of hair. I kissed her cunt with a hunger that I hadn't felt for another woman; it's always been about me getting off. Not this time. I pressed my tongue between her outer lips and traced the length of her opening until I felt the little hood just above it. Her hips twitched upward against my face, and I took that as a sign that I was on the rights. I tongued that nub until I heard noises begin. It started out as a whimpering then grew into a moan that sounded damn near pained. Maybe this wasn't enough? I pressed a finger into the growing dampness of her sex; the flowing gasp assured me I was doing well.

As soon as I got a feel of her, taking in the cues she offered with the roll of her hips and the light moans. I worked her until the aching of my cock was just too much to bear. I sat up and reached over to the bedside table to rifle through the draw until I could find a rubber. I quietly damned her demand of making me wear shorts as I shoved them off my hips so I could slide the rubber on. I spared her one look, seeing her attention focused on me had me slowing down.

"You okay?" I checked before moving forward.

Her eyes connected with mine, I could see the hesitation there. She was having second thoughts, and I felt my testicles clench, I was going to end up with a set of blue balls. Bloody fucking fantastic.

"I-I'm okay," she swallowed thickly, and for a second, I thought she was going to pull away. Wasn't shit I could do. Honestly, I'm not that kind of man. There would be no enjoyment out of trying to get this if she didn't want it, too.

"You sure?" I lay down beside her, making a point of keeping my throbbing erection far from her. I had gotten ahead of myself in my haste to get wrapped up and inside her. I was too eager, maybe that was it. Or maybe… maybe it was something else, "You're not a virgin, are you?"

She laughed, it sounds nervous for a moment before she relaxed against me. Things started to defuse. "No," she took a deep breath and seemed to be interested in touching me for the first time. Her fingers carefully started to trace lightly at the line between my pectorals. I couldn't help that they twitched in response, "I've never had a one night stand before. I've never been good with the idea of casual sex."

"Doll," I cupped her cheek. "This isn't casual sex," I saw the doubt looking back at me. What I said didn't seem to make sense. I fought for a way to explain, "This is two weeks of getting a bad man out of your system. I give you the full permission to take advantage of me at any turn you want. I'd be more than happy to be taken advantage of so you can forget that jackass you left back at home."

I kissed her gently, carefully easing against her. She responded better this time, her hand curling up my chest and around my neck to curl in my hair. There were no tense second thoughts, she felt relaxed. While the responses I'd gotten from her before hadn't been forced, or I didn't think they were, there was something more receptive to her now. Her hands wandered, touching and tracing in a way that didn't do me any favors. I took the opportunity to do the same, even after all that I had already done. My hands skimmed along her skin tracing nonsense down her back as she shifted closer.

I probably should have started with making out first, because here she was now an eager participant with every kiss and caress I made. It was hard to argue with my cock, he'd wanted her from the moment she walked in the door. When her leg edged up on my hip, it was so hard not to press my hips against her. I managed a hand between us, rubbing against her sex to see if this would go where I hoped it would. She was still wet, her hips rocked against my hand.

"I want you," I gritted out against her lips because I could only imagine how it would feel once she was wrapped around me.

"I want you," she echoed, and there was something about the whispered words that struck me in a way I wasn't prepared for.

I couldn't think about the feeling it put in my chest, I couldn't think past the feel of her against me and the throb of my dick. So, taking that as a go ahead my hand pulled from teasing her sex to grasp my prick so I could take aim. I took a slow stroke to fill her, just to be sure. I wanted to surge forward, but I didn't want to hurt her. There was this need to be gentle, to give instead of taking. I didn't know if it was because I wanted her to come back to me for more of if it was just the desire to be better than the man she left behind.

So, I made an effort to listen to every noise she made, to take a hint of every twitch and flutter of the muscles that enveloped me every time I seethed my cock into her tightness. I held onto her tightly and made no effort to fall into the instinct of just fucking her, I didn't want to come just yet. For some reason, this was to be savored, and I needed to feel her come long before I could.

I held onto her, and she clung to me as our hips moved together. We shared kisses until her head fell back, her brows drawn together as she rode out the feeling I was invoking in her. I got to see it all. I couldn't remember the last time I faced a woman while I fucked her; I was just as entertained by shoving her face first into the bed as I dove in.

Meghan was different.

I had a feeling that each time I got her to bed she would be different, too.

11

Meghan

I woke up with a distinct feeling that I wasn't in my own bed. When I opened my eyes to see an unfamiliar ceiling, it was nothing but confirmation that I wasn't home. I was comfortable and for the first time since I caught James with another woman I'd woken up feeling light and satisfied. I woke up without anything dragging me down; I didn't have the second thoughts of what I might have done wrong clouding my mind.

I stretched, taking in the ache between my thighs and the heavy weight across my waist. The night came back to me vividly, and I glanced to see Deme in the bed with me. He was on his stomach, one arm thrown over me, and the other curled up around his head. The blankets had been kicked to the point that all that was covered was his bare ass.

Considering the type of lifestyle he seemed to live, it was hard to imagine how he managed to maintain the definition. I spotted scratches on his shoulders, and I felt my cheeks burn. Had it been that intense? I don't think we had done anything out of the ordinary, save for when he buried his face between my legs. But I had held on to him hard enough to leave marks. Maybe it was because it was something I needed, that's the way I felt.

James had always been selfish, going only as long as he was entertained. Last night I had been put first, and he had made a point of making me at ease. There had been a point where he promised me that he would get James out of my system.

Two weeks of this? I don't know that I could handle it every night, but I think I could be won over.

I took the time to study his relaxed face; it was turned in my direction and mostly obscured by the pillow. His thick brows were slack, and his olive skin did little to hide the dark circles under his eyes. He probably had plenty of nights where he stayed out too late and drank until he crashed. There wasn't anything to commit to here. That wasn't something I wanted, sure I might still be young, but I didn't want to take everything I've built back at home and throw it away for some pretty man that liked to party a little too much.

If I can attract this man then I will be okay, I decided. *I will survive.*

I needed to get up and get a shower. I didn't have a clue as to what time it was, but I didn't want to be in his bed when he woke up. There would probably be an awkward conversation that I'd rather not participate in. So, I carefully wiggled out from under the arm that had been thrown over me, and when he didn't seem to react, I turned to sit on the edge of the bed. I stopped when I realized I didn't have any clothes in here to cover myself with. I doubted that he'd sleep through me stripping the bed of the sheet to cover myself.

What happened to the shirt I had on when I first came in here? He wouldn't miss it if I borrowed it again. I gave the floor a cursory look before determining that it wasn't there. *Maybe it is lost somewhere in the sheets?*

"You could just stay in bed," it was grunted out like he was stretching as he spoke. Then I felt the bed shift, I turned to see him roll over and I couldn't help but look over the view it presented me with. "Or," he released a breath. "You can walk out naked. That's a show I'd watch without complaint." He paused and rubbed a hand over his face as if he was trying wake himself up, "Except for the part where you'd be walking out. Everything okay, love?"

Deme was a picture of temptation, even with sleep clouding his face. Modesty, I knew from our first meeting, wasn't a concern of his. He was completely on display without even bothering to cover the erection that was nestled between his thighs. It made my face grow hotter, and I had to jerk my eyes away from him, so I didn't find myself crawling back to him.

"Everything's fine," I assured him. "I need a shower; I think I've spent enough time in bed." I decided the best bet would probably to not look at him at all. I couldn't be seduced by the sight of him if I didn't look at him. "We can't stay in bed all day."

"Can't we? Isn't this a vacation for you?" he hummed as if he understood what I wasn't saying.

"It is," I stood and tried to not cover myself and failed. I didn't have the confidence that he did. I ended up crossing my arms over my breasts. "But I'm going to get clean and comfortable." I couldn't stand before him like that any longer because I knew he was studying me like I had him. I didn't give him long to look. Instead, I walked out of the master bedroom to find my own room.

"Bugger all," I heard as I made my way down the hallway. "I'm in trouble."

12

Demetri

It took me a little while to understand that when Meghan said she was going to get comfortable that she was going to need space. I tried not to let it bother me. I don't know what I expected, but I had hoped it would be different.

It was depressing to be in a house with another person and feel alone. But, I tried to respect her needs. I think the worst part was the fact that I hadn't expected the fact that I needed to see her and I wanted her to feel the same. I only got to see her at meals, and then the conversation was limited in favor of actually eating.

How did I get myself into this? I probably would have been better off going to Colorado when she first got here instead of sitting here, out on the back patio, waiting for her to deem to give me the slightest bit of attention. And this was just after fucking her once. Would it be any different if I were to bed her again? Or would I just be stuck pining for more even after that?

I didn't know what to do. I had been so keen on rebelling against what my parents wanted that I never tried to build any sort of connection with any of the women I was with. Was it because I felt bad for her? Is that it?

I looked at the newspaper blankly, trying to decipher the words but they only seemed to bleed together. Maybe this was my punishment for being a whore. I was about to give up and go see what I could do for just a bit of her company until I heard footsteps come out onto the patio. I looked up, and my heartbeat picked up.

She was wearing a modest bikini top and a pair of bright pink shorts that exposed a healthy length of her thighs. Her hair was tied up on the top of her head, and she looked down at me, with sunglasses on as if she didn't have a clue about what she was doing to me.

"Mind if I join you?"

I was ready to scoot over so she'd have room on the same lounge as I until I saw her take a seat in the opposite one. Of course. I felt like an ass, but she didn't seem to notice.

"Make yourself at home." That was a stupid thing to say.

She shot me a smile and eased back on the cushion of the lounge. "It's beautiful today," she released a sigh as she started to take in the sun. I assumed her eyes were closed behind her glasses.

"It is," I agreed, though I hadn't been looking at the beach or the clear skies above us. She had my full undivided attention. I waited a beat, just watching her take in the sun and trying my damnedest to not seem like a desperate imbecile. "You good?"

"You're worried about me?"

"Well," I settled back on my own lounge and made a show of looking at the paper I had been struggling with before she joined me. "I figure I got reason enough for it. You renting out my place, and then us having a moment. I'm just trying to determine if I need to worry." I was being mostly honest, but I at least managed a cool air as I said it. I didn't want her to get the hint that I wanted her again, though I didn't have a clue how observant she was.

"You don't need to worry," she released a breath. "You're the kind of guy a girl can get in trouble with."

I couldn't help but laugh because she didn't even know. "You could get in trouble with me?"

She snorted, and I had to put my paper down, I couldn't pretend to look at it anymore. I had to look at her. Even in the sunlight she had her own shine. I felt like a moth drawn to a flame just looking at her.

"Look at you," she propped her sunglasses up on the top of her head as she spoke, so I got a glimpse of the blue eyes beneath them. "You're far too attractive for me. I could easily be played by you, and I don't know that there's anything I could do to stop it."

I saw what she was saying, and it didn't make me feel any better. The only thing I could think was to continue on the path I had offered when we were together. But I knew when it was time for us to part ways I would probably find it hard to let her go.

"I won't break your heart," I said after a beat. "I don't want to." It sounded like the truth because it was. "You can have fun without committing to more than that." After the night at the club, I knew that whatever we did I wouldn't be just having fun with her. I could see myself getting attached.

"Look," she sat up and turned towards me. "Fun is one thing, but--"

"I'm clean," I said without letting her finished. "You've got nothing to worry about from me. You don't get this," I gestured back towards the house. "By being stupid." Granted, this wasn't the fruit of my efforts by any means. She didn't need to know that. She didn't need to know who I was; with Americans they didn't really pay much attention to the monarchies of the world. I doubt if I told her she would be able to point my country out on the map.

It would be safer to just let her assume that I was wealthy and that I had somehow amassed this money on my own. It was a little white lie that didn't matter. This would be a limited thing, a fling. It was all it could be.

Her lips twisted up as she studied me, I didn't know if she could see my thoughts on my face. If she was going to call me an ass or not. Instead, she came to sit beside me on the lounge I was relaxed on.

"Let's not be stupid then," her voice was low, and it cut into me. Like she cast a spell on me that I couldn't shake. I didn't want to shake it. Not with the way that she leaned into me, I didn't give her the opportunity to kiss me first. I was so starved that I caught her lips first.

It'd only been two days, but when I kissed her, it felt like it had been too long. I was electrified by every touch, every kiss she returned.

I was so fucked.

13

Meghan

"I think I'm making a mistake," I was in the guest room I had chosen to stay in, that I hadn't been sleeping in lately. After the first night of sleeping with Deme, he would find ways to talk me into coming to his bed. On a night I had elected to try to sleep alone he ended up coming in to curl around me like a cat.

"Just to sleep," he murmured against my neck. But there was something about his scent, the feel of his skin, that had awakened my body to the point that we did more than just sleep.

"Why do you say that?" Jodie asked, her tone sounded as if she wasn't taking me seriously. "You said he's hot and he's not stingy. How could it be a mistake?" I heard her sigh heavily, "Girl you need to get that other man out of your head."

"James isn't in my head," I wanted to growl at her. I flopped back on the bed I hadn't slept alone in days.

"No? Then what's the problem?"

"This guy is winning and dining me," I snapped at her. "He's being attentive and caring. How am I going to be able to walk away from this in a week?" I didn't want to go into details about the sex, I didn't want to give her an idea just how good it was.

"Oh," she released a breath as she finally seemed to catch on. "You're catching feelings for him. Baby, you're supposed to use this guy as a rebound. You're not supposed to fall for him." I groaned and rolled over, letting the phone fall on the bed. She was being rough with her way of thinking. I never liked the idea of using people and with the way Deme had been treating me he didn't deserve the title of being rebound. "If it's that bad," her voice was loud enough for me to understand what she said without the speaker to my ear. "Girl, how did you make it this far in life without getting run over by every guy you came across?"

"I've not dated a lot," I admitted because there was no reason to not be honest. Jodie wasn't someone I'd describe as a best friend, but now that I didn't have James anymore she was the closest thing I had.

"You didn't give your virginity to James, did you? I know you're small town, girl, but I hope you're not THAT small town."

"No," I groaned. "Jesus." I pinched the bridge of my nose and tried my best not to get angry. "I didn't."

"Thank God," she breathed, I didn't want to know what she had been thinking. "Look," she started again. "If he's good looking and treating you right, I can see the appeal. But you said he was from another country, right? Even if he's rich, there's a good chance that he might be trying to get a free pass to citizenship." I didn't think about that. I bit my lip and sat back up, "I'm not trying to make this out to be horrible, but maybe... maybe don't put your heart into it. It's just a fling."

"I've never had one before," I admitted, I didn't want to tell her that I hadn't had a lot of relationships. I found it hard to open up to people, so it wasn't often that I did have a lot of relationships under my belt. I've only had one one night stand, and I regretted it immensely. So far, I wasn't regretting what I was doing. But this couldn't end on a high note.

"Oh I see," she sounded irritated now. "You're getting attached. Look," she paused as if she was considering a gentler way to put this. "He's probably in the idea that this is purely a fling. If you don't believe me give him your phone number when it's time to leave. If he wants to make it serious, he'll keep in touch. If not...

well, there you go. At least you won't have as much invested in him that you did with James."

I digested what she said, biting my lip. It would solve things, answer questions at the end of the week. But, it wouldn't help me now. "What do I do until then?"

The silence was my answer for a beat like she couldn't figure out what I should do. "Enjoy yourself," she said quietly. "Take what he's offering and enjoy yourself."

I guess there was nothing more than I could do. I ended the call and made an excuse of flicking through emails and social media to keep myself busy. I needed space to ride out the sudden vulnerable feeling that I had. Jodie hadn't understood, at least I didn't think she did. She wasn't really the type to have her heart on her sleeve. She didn't realize the more time I spent with Deme, the more he worked his way into mine.

A knock cut through my worries and brought my attention to the subject of them. He was leaning against the door frame wearing a pair of sweats and looking so irresistible. How'd I managed to look at him the first day and not fall into his bed?

"You alright, love?" he looked genuinely concerned. His dark brows drawn up as he looked at me, I worried for a second he had heard the conversation.

I shook off my fears and stood up, "I'm good. Did you want something?"

He shrugged, looking a picture of nonchalance. "I was hoping you would like to accompany me on a night in? Perhaps recommend a movie or two?"

"If you want to go out you don't have to stay here on my account," I set my phone aside and leveled him a look. Maybe he felt the need to entertain me, I didn't know, and I hadn't had the idea to question it at all. I had been so distracted by the attention he had been giving me that I hadn't even considered it before now. "You don't have to change what you were doing before I got here just to keep me entertained."

His dark eyes narrowed, and then he shook his head, "I want a night in. Christmas is in a couple of days, and I figured we could watch movies. Unless you have something you'd rather be doing?"

I had resigned myself to spending the holiday alone and I was prepared to spend this vacation alone wallowing. But I hadn't had the chance to do much of that. He'd occupied all of my time so far.

"What are you doing?" I asked numbly.

Confusion clouded his features, "Trying to find a way to get you on the couch to watch a movie halfway through so I can then distract you and hopefully get lucky?" He scratched his head, though he didn't even mush the artfully spiked hair that managed to make bedhead look sexy. "Did you not want to do that? I guess I might have been a little bit too needy with it," he offered me a shrug. "Sorry. I was enjoying myself. I thought you were, too?"

That's just what it was, sex and nothing else. I swallowed hard and nodded because I had been enjoying myself. I was getting attached so I tried to keep from showing the feelings on my face. I met his confusion with a shrug, and I forced a smile. "It's fine," my voice wavered. "If you want to go ahead and pick out the movie I'll be there in a minute."

I waited for him to leave because I needed to break down. I felt foolish for thinking there was something here when there wasn't. I had envisioned something coming from this, and there wasn't a chance it would. I wasn't able to rebound off of Deme. At the end of the week, I was going to slink back home worse off than I left it.

Instead of leaving, he watched me. His eyes narrowed, and he came into the room uninvited, sitting next to me on the bed like it was okay.

"It's not fine," he pointed out gently. "What's wrong?"

I wanted to glare at him, "I'd rather not--"

"Nope," he leaned against me, and it felt like he was weaseling his way in. "What's wrong?"

I should have ignored him. I should have let it play its way out and then just go home and lick my wounds like I would have had to do when I noticed James was gone. Only now, instead of pining over James, I would be pining over this man.

"What are you doing?" It came out with heat. "You know what happened to me, but here you are. You're treating this like it's some sort of relationship when it has no chance of being that." I choked a little on the words, and I wiped viciously at my face because a tear had trickled down. I didn't want to cry in front of him, but it wasn't something that I seemed to have any control over.

He stayed quiet, didn't move as he seemed to take in what I'd said. Maybe my emotions were getting the best of him, too. I didn't want to look at him, it was bad enough that I'd been driven to this and I had lost control of it. Despite the appearance that he cared, I was still raw. The prospect of facing it all over again just made me pull away.

"Why do this?" I demanded more than asked.

"I thought," his voice was low as he started to speak. "I thought maybe I could help," he swore then I felt him flop backward on the bed. "That's a lie. I saw you," his voice rumbled lightly. "And I wanted you. That much should've been obvious."

"Just sex then," I breathed. I felt so stupid. Of course, it was just that.

"It could be that," he said in a gentle tone. "It would be easier if it were just that."

"How would it be easy?" I demanded, turning to glare at him. "Why would it be easier?" There was something about what he said that made me angry. "Oh, you think I would want to sleep with you just for your money is that it? You think I'm upset about the prospect of this just being about sex because I want your fucking money?"

"No," he sat up and seemed like he was trying to quell my anger, but it was too late.

I stood, turning back to him. Being used by another man just wasn't something I wanted to let go. The fire, the anger over everything I've dealt with up to this point was something I had a hold of and I wasn't letting go.

"I don't want your fucking money," I snapped back at him. "I've got this far without it, and I don't need it now," he looked surprised at me, his mouth opened as if he were going to say something and I didn't give him the chance. "I've put enough aside for people," I turned away and started for the door. "I've sacrificed enough of my own happiness for other people. Thanks for your cruel attempt to make me feel better. I would have been better off without it. I'll expect the rest of the money I spent on this God forsaken vacation in my account before the New Year, or I'll be speaking with a lawyer." I left it at that and started to stalk out of the room, I had had enough of all of it. I was going to go home, and if James wasn't out of the apartment by the time I got there, I'd make sure he got out.

"Wait," I heard him cry out, but I needed to get away. I didn't want to break down in front of him. I was bound and determined to let this anger see me through to the front door. I didn't have a clue as to where I would go from there. I envisioned myself heading to the airport when I first started the tirade. I was halfway down the hallway before he caught up with me, his arms around me halting my escape. "Wait," his voice was heavier now. "You don't get to start a serious conversation like that and walk out."

"You've made it clear what you want," I snapped and fought his hold on me.

"I said it would be easier if that was just it," he growled into my ear. He tightened his hold on me, and I knew there wasn't a chance I would be getting loose. "Where can this go, Meghan?" Him saying my name struck a note, I'd been nothing but pet names before. "You leave and then what? Tell me what sense you can make of it going?"

I didn't have an answer because I didn't know. I couldn't think of how this would go, I didn't know where he was from or how long distance would even work. I just could feel the hold he had on me now and the strangling hold that was on my heart. I just knew I couldn't leave him as if I felt nothing for him.

"I want you," his voice slid through my ear and despite my anger made me quake. "I would like nothing more than to take you home with me and keep you," his voice lowered. "Would you give up everything to stay here with me? Hm?"

"Oh, so you can just use me instead?" I stomped on his foot in an effort to shake him. "That's a better idea?"

He winced but didn't let go. If anything his arms tightened around me, "I thought maybe we could gather mutual enjoyment from it." He released a breath then shifted his stance, "I didn't expect you to get attached."

There was something about the way he said it that seemed to sap all of the fight out of me. I went limp in his arms and just let him hold onto me. "If you didn't want me to get attached why give me so much attention?"

I found myself choking a little bit as I tried to smother my tears, "Why be so attentive?"

I didn't get an answer at first. If anything all he did was shift me into a better position to carry me, and then carted me to the living room. Deme deposited me on the couch, and then he settled in beside me. His hand stayed on my knee as if that would keep me there if I decided to run.

"I want you," he said though it sounded uneasy now. His confidence seemed to go with my desire to fight. "I can't think past that."

"You've had me," I point out glumly. I didn't want to point out how frequently it'd been that he had me. He'd been there. He knew.

"Yea well," he looked away and had the courtesy to look uncomfortable. "It's not been enough."

That didn't help anything. If anything he was just making everything more confusing. "What do you want?"

I watched as he took both hands into his hair, his expression twisted up as he seemed to think about my question. He didn't look at me. Instead, he seemed to be fixed on the elaborately carved coffee table in front of us.

"Can we just," he waved a hand. "Keep on like we have been. Just ride it out. Let me be with you and enjoy your company, fuck you until neither of us can see straight and leave it at that?"

"And what happens when I have to go?" My voice was shaky. While the idea of doing what he wanted had its appeal, it still left a whole lot of unanswered questions. He wanted me, but did he care? Would he miss me when I was gone? Did his heart speed up to the point it was painful when we were together? It felt like I was on a high when he slid into bed with me and settled up behind me.

He still didn't look at me. His hands dropped, and he continued to look hard at the coffee table. "I hadn't thought that far ahead. I figured if I ignored our impending separation that it wouldn't happen. I dunno, maybe you'd elect to stay. Something like that." I didn't know what to say to that. He wasn't serious, was he? "I've made a point," he finally looked at me, meeting my gaze without fully turning towards me. "To not get serious with the girls that I see. It's easier to keep an emotional distance. I don't do relationships."

"I wish I could say I worked the same way," this was clue enough to me as to how this would go. No matter how much longer I decided to stay with him, I'd still end up going home in the same shape I was in when I got here. Or worse.

"I can't offer you a serious relationship," his voice was gentle.

I nodded, that much was obvious. "I can't stay here and fool myself," I said evenly.

His expression went blank, and he looked away from me, "I don't want you to leave."

I didn't know how to respond to that. I opened my mouth to argue but was cut off. It sounded as if someone was jiggling the doorknob to the front door. I looked between Deme and the front door; he'd turned to give it his attention, too.

"The chef?" I offered as my only guess.

He shook his head and stood, by now whoever was at the door had decided to knock heavily on it. I got a look from him before he went to it. His demeanor managed to change. He went from confused, but still managing a sexy air, to dark. Did he think I called someone? He got to the door and managed the locks, once it opened his attempt at being intimidating changed. I stood to get a better look.

"Demetri," another woman snapped. "I had to come all the way out here because you wouldn't answer your damned phone," she huffed and shoved past him to stalk into the foyer. "Your tantrum is over here and now!"

It made sense now. How could I not see it? I stared at him, my heart sinking into my stomach.

"You're married," I cried to myself.

Whatever had been going on between them came to a screaming halt as they both turned to look at me. I immediately noticed the similarities in their facial features. Deme's face twisted in disgust and he looked as if he might be ill, "Fucking no! This is my sister!"

The woman snorted and looked back to Deme, "This is what you are here doing?" There was a frown on her full lips, and I was intimidated by just how beautiful this woman was. She was slimmer than I and had the same tan complexion and rich chocolate hair that her brother did. "A woman? This is what you are hiding from mother?"

"I'm not hiding her," he snapped at her. "We just met a week ago. There's nothing to hide."

The woman came to me as if he hadn't spoken and offered me a hand. "Hello." There was something about her accent that seemed more cultured than Deme's. I couldn't place the origin, though it had something to with my lack of familiarity with European countries. Or that's where I assumed he was from. "I am Nadine Hass. Demetri's older sister."

"Meghan Reed," I took her hand and shook it. I didn't know where to go from here. So, the best thing I could think to do was accept the introduction and offer one of my own.

"I'm fucking firing Maurice," Deme stated with venom.

"You are pretty," his sister responded with a slight smile, obviously ignoring her brother. "I can see your appeal. But why hide you?"

"It's been a week," I shrugged helplessly.

"Oh?" She looked disappointed. "So, he didn't whisk away to be with you?"

I shook my head, hating to be the bearer of bad news at any time. "I rented this place, and he was here when I got here," I gave her another helpless shrug. "He didn't want to leave, and I suppose I just didn't kick up a big enough fuss to get him to."

I watched Nadine turn to Deme to glare at him, he didn't appear to be cowed by her expression. "So why are you here?"

He shook his head and folded his arms over his bare chest. I felt terrible for having confronted him like I did, but I still felt rubbed raw despite his attempt to soothe my bruised heart. Had I known his sister was going to come knocking on the door I probably would have saved my worries, or not brought them up at all.

"I wasn't going to sit through another party where they try to pawn me off on whatever woman they deem good enough," he cut himself off and gave me a look before looking back to his sister. "For whatever it is they want me to do."

That rewarded me another curious look from his sister. Her lips pursed and she raised her brow at me, it was an unspoken question that I didn't understand.

"She doesn't know?" Deme's sister whispered, but was still loud enough for me to hear.

His face crumpled, "I didn't have a reason to tell her." He turned from me like he couldn't look at me. "So, I didn't tell her."

My stomach twisted, it was obvious enough that he wasn't married. But I couldn't take the confusion of listening to their conversation. "Tell me what?"

Deme shook his head as if he was trying to dismiss my question, but Nadine spoke up instead. "Crown Prince Demetri Hass of Ashouvania," she announced with authority. She even did a pronounced curtsey as if she was bestowing him a great honor by announcing his identity.

I sat back down heavily on the couch, dumbfound. "Prince?"

14

Demetri

I didn't think the night could get worse, but I could see that it found a way to in the shape of my sister and her smug introduction she gave. Any chances I had of salvaging what I had going on with Meghan was crushed by Nadine. Looking at Meghan's shocked face said enough as to what kind of woman she was, she was surprised to learn about who I really was. I didn't have anything to say, I couldn't think of a word that might offer her any sort of comfort.

I was an ass. I doubted I could have kept it a secret if I would have entertained the relationship she seemed to want. If I'd been smart, I would have kept to myself or left.

So, I wasn't only an ass, I was a dumb one.

"Why are you here?" I didn't look at Nadine when I asked it. I was too distracted by what this would mean and where things would go from here with Meghan. I wasn't ready to let go of the woman, I didn't want to abandon the feelings she had invoked in me.

"Father commanded that you stop your sulking and come home," Nadine said simply. "You have duties to the crown, and you have shirked them long enough."

I never wanted to throttle my sister so much as I had at that moment, "So instead of sending a message, you come to do father's bidding?"

"Send a message? To whom? The phone you are ignoring?"

"Like you can't get a message to the people that run this house or any of the other houses we have around the world," I huffed irritated with her. "Give me some sort of notice, so I don't do something stupid," I snapped as I started building my tirade. "Maybe I left because I didn't want to participate in any of it." I wasn't done sulking, I wasn't done with Meghan. I didn't want to go back home and submit to the commands of growing up and settling down. "You might as well go home and tell father I said fuck off."

I heard the crack before I felt the impact of my sister slapping me; she hit me just hard enough for it to make noise. The sting was just enough to make my cheek twitch. "You," her voice was hard, I'd made her mad, "are overstepping. Stop being a spoiled little brat."

Meghan had looked away, though I imagine she was just as surprised by the sudden bout of violence as I was. "I'll leave you two to your discussion," Meghan said quietly as if her movement wouldn't draw attention to herself.

Meghan was far more important than anything Nadine may have had to say. I wanted nothing more to follow her down the hallway and try to explain. I shouldn't need to do that, but I wanted her to understand. Just like I wanted her to let me be with her.

"Why the hell do you have to come ruin everything?" I yelled but didn't look back to my sister, "Why can't you be Crown Princess instead? You're the favorite. I'll always be the disappointment."

"Too late," she snorted at me. "If I was the favorite and we were ready to make that leap into the modern world I would not have been married off to Abir," she didn't offer me any sort of sympathy. "So if you want to take this girl home with you and offer her up to mother and father, I think they are to the point where they are so tired of your resisting that they would not care who you brought home as long as you did come home."

I grimaced at that, because while the idea of having more time with Meghan had its appeal, I didn't think I was ready to offer up to something I didn't know I even wanted.

"Marriage has to be involved?" I rubbed at my stomach, feeling it twist and bubble at just the idea.

It was only then that my sister's features softened and she looked more like the girl that I had played with as a child. The girl I whose hair I'd pull when I was bored and dolls that I would destroy when I was angry at her. I had followed her like a shadow, mostly because of the fact that she was older and knew so much more than I did.

"Marriage is not so bad," she smiled at me, a face I was as familiar with as if it were my own. We were years apart, but I'll be damned if I didn't still look up to her, even if I had more than a few inches on her. "You might find that having someone beside you, caring for you, so you are not facing things alone to be nice. Like whatever brought you here," she heaved a sigh. "And the fact that I will be dragging you back kicking and screaming if I have to."

Well, that was good to know. "By yourself?" I could take her, we both knew it too as we'd gotten into scrapes often enough when puberty hit.

"You think it would be that easy?" She gave me a dazzling smile; this was something she found funny. "I brought bodyguards that are okay with carrying you out to the car and throwing you in the trunk. Might be because of your pension for pranks that I had more than a few volunteer for the job."

"Can we put this off for a day?" I motioned towards the hallway, thinking of Meghan. "I have a mess to clean up. I was in the middle of something when you barged in." I didn't want to leave on a bad note with her, even if she was upset by the little bit of me she learned. The idea of leaving her heartbroken just made my chest feel tight.

"There's a plane waiting," Nadine shook her head. "You cannot put it off anymore. I am not waiting a day for you to patch things up with your girlfriend."

I bared my teeth at her because if anyone knew how to push my buttons, it was my sister. I didn't have any claims on Meghan, but the idea of calling her mine wasn't something I hadn't entertained. It'd always been a passing idea, especially with the way that she had felt lying in bed beside me. "She's not--" I started to argue.

"If it's that important to you," she cut me off and began to move down the hallway after Meghan. "Bring her with you," she tapped on the door to the guest room--her room when we were younger. "Meghan," she called out and offered her a brilliant smile that could sway just about anyone. "Darling we have a plane to catch. Pack your bag."

"What?" Meghan asked as she peeked from the doorway. I could hear her confusion, and I followed, I didn't try to deter my sibling's tactics at all. Though, really, I should have stepped in and stopped it. "Pack my bag? I have another week booked here."

"A week booked?" I got a look from Nadine; it was something near a glower. "Do not worry, darling. We are not kicking you out. But, we have a plane to catch."

"A plane?" Meghan looked to me like I could explain my sister's thought process. I shrugged at her but didn't offer any sort of explanation.

"Demetri has something important he needs to see to," Nadine spoke as she went into the bedroom like Meghan wasn't there. "He is worried about leaving you here. We have plenty of room, so there is no reason to," she found Meghan's bag and without much concern about her privacy seemed to go about ensuring her things were in it. She frowned a little, "Well. It is going to be way too cold for you to wear any of this. Do you anything more appropriate for a colder climate?"

"I have an outfit," she started to say before shaking her head. "I don't need to go with you. My vacation is almost over," she looked at me for help. "I don't understand what's going on?"

"Do not worry about your vacation," my sister had her ways. "Consider this just an extension. Come on now," Nadine wasn't offering any room for argument, this was her skill.

After a minute of watching, Meghan began to help her pack even with the confusion as to what was going on. At last, she asked, "Where are we going?"

"Ashouvania," Nadine enunciated each syllable slowly so that it was clear what she was said. She then zipped up Meghan's suitcase and walked out of the room with it. "Come on now, let us get to the car, so we are not arriving home too late," she commanded in her pleasant tone as she brushed passed me.

"Do I have a choice in this?" Meghan eyed me. "You're not kidnapping me, are you?"

"Of course you do," I tried to keep my tone light. "Diplomatic immunity only goes so far," it was supposed to be a joke. She didn't laugh. I cleared my throat; I was alone with her and now was the chance to say so many things. Instead, I was cracking jokes like an ass. "You could consider it as a means of me paying you back for ruining your vacation," I offered. I didn't have a choice as Nadine had plainly put it with the threat of armed guards throwing me in the trunk. I wanted the opportunity to speak with Meghan. If I had to open up and show her everything what better place than doing it at home? "Do you want to go?" Did she want to see me for what I really was? I wasn't ready to show that to someone, I could admit that, but the choice was now out of my hands.

Meghan hesitated, the talk we had before probably coming back to her. "I don't have a passport," she admitted after a beat. "I've never traveled outside of the country."

"Don't worry about the passport," I assured her. "We have a private flight. It will be handled." At least I assumed it would be, Nadine wasn't one to ignore the details. Right now the only detail I was concerned about was right in front of me. "If you want to go?"

The hesitation was still there, but I watched as she nodded. I felt an odd sense of relief, and if it wasn't for Nadine calling for us to hurry from the front door, I probably would have pushed forward into the room. It was hard to not be drawn to her; I doubted having her home would put a damper on that.

15

Meghan

I shouldn't have done this. I should have never agreed to this. There was something about getting on the plane that seemed to make good sense finally settle in. It was extremely obvious as soon as we boarded the little jet that Deme actually being a prince wasn't a joke. While we drove to the airport, I did my best to do an internet search the name she called him. Of course, Deme was short for Demetri. For some reason, I was still hung up on calling him Deme, even in my head. I managed to find a few short articles, and there was even a Wikipedia dedicated to the country. There was a list of its current monarchy; Alard and Edda Hass. It even listed Deme and his sister as their children. There was a small history that involved a few skirmishes during the Second World War and the trade of ore from the sentiment rich mountains that took up the majority of the little country.

From there I found articles about Deme, one mentioned an Oxford education and a long list of achievements that made me dizzy. Here I was just a paralegal, and I had no hopes of offering any sort of comparison. I didn't even get a four-point-o grade point average in community college. I didn't have anything to offer this guy at all. What the hell was I doing?

I should have put my foot down and just let them leave without me. I should have told that sweet, but pushy, woman that she could leave with her brother and I would be staying the rest of my vacation there. Alone. But maybe that's the reason why I let her drag me along. I didn't want to be alone, especially not on Christmas, just days away.

Maybe that was why Deme was lingering close by. He didn't seem opposed to the idea of me going with them. It seemed safe enough, but I still found myself texting Jodie a short run down as to what was happening. Just in case. Though the joke about diplomatic immunity did raise some hairs, I figured the worse that I could walk away from this with was a long plane ride home, alone. A free trip to abroad would normally be too good to pass up. I should be eager about this. But from the moment we got into the limousine, my nerves were on edge. Second thoughts were assaulting me at every turn, but I never worked up the courage to tell them I didn't want to go.

Nadine spoke animatedly as she went to work on her phone. She sat across from me by a massive muscular man that I could only assume was a guard. She started asking me questions, "This is just to make sure we do not have any hiccups once we have to go through customs. Demetri mentioned you did not have a passport. I'm just making sure everything will go smoothly." She gave me a wink as if it would set me at ease.

It didn't.

I stayed close to Deme out of habit. Even though I wasn't sure where we stood, I felt a certain air of comfort just by being close to him. He didn't seem to protest it at all. When he led me out to the little jet that would take us to his country, he took my hand. The jet had an unfamiliar crest on the side of it, and my nerves were in an uproar as we boarded. If it weren't for the tight grip he had on my hand, I might have tried to run for it.

"You Okay?" He looked at me as if he knew what I was feeling.

I don't know what I could have said to him. I was still surprised that I was making this leap with strangers. Well, he was a prince... kind of a stranger. The fact that we had slept together on a number of occasions didn't seem to matter.

"Where does this go from here?" I whispered it because while there weren't a lot of people on the plane, I didn't want to question this loud enough for the others to hear.

Instead of looking surprised or disturbed like he had before, he smiled at me. "Let's ride it out," he suggested as he started to lead me towards the spacious rows of seats. He offered me the window seat before he settled down beside me. "See where it goes, eh?"

Honestly, that's was more than I expected from him. It struck me speechless, and I could only offer him a nod. Did I really want to stick around with him? He hadn't openly lied to me... unless you count omission.

His closeness had a way of making me feel comfortable all the while sending my heart racing at the same time. Was this normal? I couldn't recall feeling like this with James if there was ever a time he made my heart race I couldn't remember. I found myself trying to make comparisons between two men that didn't compare at all. Even with the sudden news of just who he was. It brought to my attention just how much I didn't know about him.

"Were you going to tell me at all?" I decided to ask.

He looked away from me, and I thought back to the conversation we had before we were interrupted. He hadn't looked at me then, he hadn't been sure just what he intended to do. It had all stemmed on what was supposed to be a one night stand. How did it grow into more than that?

"I didn't think that far ahead," he admitted, breaking through the downward spiral of my thoughts. "A fault," he leaned back into the leather seat. "I don't think ahead and prefer to be in the now," he grunted a little. "I usually ignore the consequences."

"That's why you were in Miami?"

"No," he shrugged a little. Not meeting my gaze, but speaking in a way that I knew he wasn't spinning lies to me. "I came to the States because I've been in an ongoing argument with my parents because I am," he grimaced. "Crown Prince..." the tone he used was twisted in disgust, "of my country. I'm its future. Something that's been drummed into my head since I was a child. Not something I wanted or something I chose for myself. Between the two of us," he gestured to the seats in front of us where his sister was. "She is far more capable than I am. She would be a better leader than I will ever be." He sounded depressed, and I felt pain for him. His hands went into his hair, and for the first time since I'd met him, he looked tired. Like the entire act of speaking about himself had sapped all of his energy. "I ran because I'm not ready for the responsibility."

"How old are you?" I didn't hide the grimace because this was something I should have known before the first time we were together.

The smirk he shot me showed that he was grateful for the change of questioning, but amused that I had to ask. "Twenty-eight in a few months," he didn't hide his humor. "Don't worry, love. You weren't robbing the cradle."

I snorted because that much was obvious. "Why run from responsibility at your age? If you weren't royalty, you would be going without a plan in your life and having to fit the bill for yourself." There was something about it irritated me, "I get how having everything planned out for you can be upsetting, but at least you know there's something in your future." I heaved a sigh and looked out the window, feeling the rock as the jet prepared to take off. "It's better than having nothing foreseen in your future and having to face it alone."

I didn't know how he took my opinion; I didn't bother to look at him again. Not even when the plane started to rumble as it took off. We had a brief stop in what I assumed was Atlanta for customs. The fact that we didn't have to get off the plane was something that surprised me, we were served brunch by a beautiful attendant that spoke clipped English and something that sounded like German. Or maybe Dutch? I had a hard time placing it. I felt foolish, so I let Deme speak for me. The fluid way he switched languages was impressive, as far as I could tell there was no flirting. The attendant was respectful and polite, offering me a smile as she offered me a dish.

He was so much more than I thought he was. I deftly watched him as we ate. It was just long enough for us to finish eating before the plane took off again. When Nadine stood in front of us, it was clear that this leg would be much longer. "There are beds if you would feel more comfortable sleeping," she stretched. "We have some time before we arrive home. Do me a favor, Demetri, make sure you have her sizes right, so we have appropriate clothing for her."

"Aye aye," he grunted the looked at me. "There's another bedroom," there was something in his tone that suggested something. When I looked, I could see the hunger in his expression.

It took an effort me to shake my head. "I'm comfortable right here. Feel free to go lay down if you want," I looked back out the window, enjoying the sight of the clouds wisping by over the dark ocean below us.

Much to my surprise, he didn't leave me to go find a more comfortable place to sleep. There was a grumble and a shift before he settled down. I don't know how long I spent looking out the window before I drifted off myself. Even with the occasional bit of turbulence.

I didn't travel by plane often. The trip down to Miami had been in the cramped quarters of coach. As was any other time I'd gotten onto a plane. I couldn't afford the lavish vacations that most went on because I decided to live in an expensive area. I did notice that this jet was a smoother ride than any other plane I'd been on and the seats that were much more comfortable.

I would have been content to sleep there if arms hadn't come around me. I was hefted up, and the sense of movement was enough to wake me up. I flailed and ended up hitting the person picking me up in the face.

"Ow," Deme grunted and held onto me tighter. "Stop love, it's just me."

My eyes fluttered open. The cabin was mostly dark, but there was just enough light for me to see his face. It was close to mine; after all, he had me cradled to his chest.

"What are you doing?" I snapped as I tried to slow the hammering of my heart.

"I was taking you to lie down," he grunted as he carefully turned us both around. "I was trying to be considerate," he shifted us away from the seats and to what looked like a Murphy bed. It was slightly bigger than a twin, and I didn't recall seeing it when we boarded. "Or would you rather stay asleep in the seats?"

"How much longer is the flight?" I tried to pull away, feeling awkward with him carrying me.

"We have maybe six more hours? Don't worry the attendant will wake us up when we need to get buckled in," he sat me on the bed and put his hands on his hips as he looked at me. "Unless you'd rather ride out six hours in a seat?"

I was still groggy, but I was half tempted go back to my seat. He just stood there waiting for me to make a decision. I gave in and flopped back on the bed, shifting only so I could wiggle under the blanket and sheet. They were soft, and I couldn't help but borrow further into them. I could sleep like this. The bed dipped, and the blanket shifted, it was obvious that I wasn't going to be in this bed alone.

"What are you doing?" I asked him again, throwing a glare at him over a shoulder.

"I want to sleep, too," he sounded grumpy as slid in beside me. "Scoot over then if you're not going to let me cuddle with you. I'll keep my hands to myself, begrudgingly," he shifted closer to my back, and I watched him settle down. "That alright with you?"

I didn't argue, I just settled back down. I didn't twitch when he curled into my back, his arm wound around my hip, and we both seemed to settle. It didn't take long for him to relax and the sound of his breathing was enough to force me to let go. The heat of him lulled me back to sleep.

16

Demetri

I was groggy when we arrived at the private airport just outside the countryside that the family manor took up. Manor was a loose term for it. It was made of dark stone with several towers with gothic peaks and hulking gargoyles. I remembered looking up at them as a child and wondering just which horror movie they had crawled out of. Now, though, I worried what Meghan might think when we drove up to it.

For now, we were waiting politely for her to change into clothes fit for the weather. It was a crisp thirty-degree Fahrenheit, and neither of us had packed accordingly. For me it wasn't much of a big deal, a message was sent ahead for a warm outfit to be sent out to us. For Meghan, they had to stop by a shop with her measurements so clothes could be purchased for her. I didn't get the opportunity to give them any sort of insight on what I thought she might like. Nadine had made the judgment on her own.

I huffed out a breath and watched as the condensation flared upward like smoke. Probably for the best I didn't get a choice. I'd spent the last week seeing her in shorts and tanks or nothing at all. I was still mournful of the fact that I hadn't had the opportunity to see her undressed since the last time we'd been intimate.

How long had it been? A day? Two?

I'm an ass.

At least she let me sleep next to her. I guess that was one saving grace. At least she agreed to come home with me. I wasn't going to be facing this by myself.

I rocked on the balls of my feet, trying to get the stiff leather of loafers to relax a little. Of course, they couldn't bring me a pair of bloody tennis shoes. They handed me clothing as if I were expected at a formal dinner. I should have put up more of a fight to come home. I would much rather be laying out on the lounge, soaking up the sun and enjoying a brandy with Meghan than this.

"Why did I agree to this?" I asked aloud.

"You did not have a choice," Nadine corrected me. I turned to see her and Meghan coming down the steps of the plane. "Remember, I did not give you one. I am not giving you the opportunity to run off and hide. I figured you would stick around if I brought your girlfriend with us."

I opened my mouth to correct her because I didn't think that I had any real claims on her. But then I didn't say anything. I found myself floundering, so I turned away from the two women as they descended from plane's boarding ramp. It was something Nadine could win; my fear was just of what Meghan would gather from it.

I followed them to the car, still musing over what it meant myself. It was something made my stomach feel like a lead weight had been dropped into it. I couldn't figure out why that irritated me. She hadn't led me on. If anything I led her on. I didn't even let up after she questioned me. I had insisted curling into the bed with her.

I am such a prick.

We loaded into a limousine, and it was a short ride to the manor. The sinking feeling only got worse; I knew what the assumption would be when she was introduced. They would probably assume that she was the reason why I buggered off, to begin with. They'd be wrong, of course, but I wasn't regretting the decision to stay in Miami when she first showed up. I wasn't regretting the night she came into my bedroom in just my shirt, because I wanted her then just like I wanted her now.

I was regretting that conversation I had with her before Nadine rudely interrupted us. Maybe if I had the bollocks, I'd been able to own up to the fact that I wanted her. If I hadn't been such a coward, I wouldn't get frightened by her asking where this was going. I didn't know where it was going and I didn't know if it had the possibility to go anywhere. I could think of a few better things to say now that didn't occur to me yesterday.

Hindsight is a bitch.

Meghan was too caught up in looking out the windows, even though there was nothing but boring countryside filled with trees and shrubs. It was the early morning hours, so I wasn't sure what she was expecting to see, but I didn't bother to ask. There was something about the open curiosity that she had that kept her pressed to the window that I couldn't try to pull her away from it.

"I promise," I said as low as I could so only she would hear. "To take you exploring while you're here."

I got a smile, it was hesitant and obvious she didn't know what to make of my promise. "I'd like that," she admitted to me just as quietly.

It felt like the right thing to do, I nodded and pulled out my phone to give myself a reminder. "We're a small country, but it's beautiful," I murmured to her. "I hope you will enjoy your stay here." I stopped there because it made it evident that she was here for a limited time. Soon I would have to let her go back to her life, and I would be stuck here.

It was a sobering thought.

Is there a way to get her to stay? What girl in her right mind wouldn't want to stay with a prince? What the fuck am I thinking? Get her to stay here?

What the fuck do I want?

The questions just seemed to swirl through my head. I didn't even see the rear gate as we came across it, but I heard Meghan gasp out in wonder as she looked up at the castle that I had grown up in. It didn't offer me any kind of distraction from the heaviness in my gut. If anything seeing the spires of the towers just made it worse.

It had been months since I ran. I hopped around Europe before I decided to just spend the winter in one of the warmest places we had a holiday home in. I spent a little over a month there before she barged in.

I rubbed at my chest through the crisp button down that I'd been given. Everything was revolving around my escaping and running into Meghan. Now both ended with me being back home. The only thing I could hope to come out of this with was some sort of sanity.

The car rolled to a halt. I probably wasn't going to get even that. I got out of the car immediately and turned, offering a hand to Meghan so she could easily get out of it and then to my sister. My gentlemanly upbringing was kicking in. All the whoring around I did was shaken off by the biting wind.

"We are expected for dinner," Nadine said as she led the way into the main foyer. She turned to Miss Janseen, the woman that had run the castle for as long as I could remember. "Miss Reed will need a room and her things should be taken up there."

"I want it as close to my room as possible," I grumped, I knew I couldn't make the demand that she stay in mine, not to Miss Janseen.

It still got the old woman's her attention, and she adjusted the frames of her glasses onto further up her nose and looked hard at Meghan. Then she looked back at me, an eyebrow raised. "Of course, shall I show her the way to it now?" Her accent was thick, and I hoped that it would be easy for Meghan to understand.

But the prospect of the woman that took a major part in raising me taking the woman I was sleeping with away made me uncomfortable. The other option was to take her with me to meet with my parents. That sounded like a worse idea. I grimaced and nodded to her, "Don't give her the fifth, please."

"I wasn't going to," I was scoffed at as she took Meghan up the flight of stairs that curved into the foyer. "Your father is expecting you. You know where he is?"

I nodded because at this time of day there was one of two places he could be. I doubted he would be in the study, he would hold more power on his throne glowering down at me. I started through the main hall until I noticed Nadine was still in the foyer, typing furiously on her phone.

"You aren't going to come gloat as I get lectured?" I asked.

"I am trying to see about getting her money refunded to her," she glared at her phone. "The website that the Amelia Island house is rented through is being difficult." She looked up at me to give me a sour look, "This is something you should have done when she got there, and you decided to get intimate with her."

"How did you find out about it?" I rubbed my neck, stalling.

"Something you said, I put two and two then did some digging," she started forward, moving without bothering to look where she was going. "Enough looking for reasons to dodge, father. You are going to have to do this now. Otherwise, he will come looking for you, and it will be much worse."

I grunted and let her lead the way, "I forgot. I didn't expect to get attached." I wasn't even thinking, "See if you can do anything about her return flight from Miami, too, will you?"

She halted just before getting to the double doors
that led into where our father held court, "You got
attached?"

I tried my best to play it off, straightening the
button down and adjusting the pea coat. "Isn't it obvious?
That's why you cornered her into agreeing to go, isn't it?"

"Honestly, I have been waiting for you to speak
up and correct me. I figured when I referred to her as
your girlfriend that you would say something," she looked
genuinely surprised. "I thought that was why you did not
bother to see to it that she got refunded."

"I called Charlie in an attempt to run her off in
the beginning," I spoke up in defense of myself. I didn't
like the idea of her assuming the worse.

"Charlie?" she looked confused. "You mean
Grant?"

"Yea," I shrugged because I didn't see it as
important.

I watched her roll her eyes as she opened one
door and peered in. When she turned back to me there
was disdain on her expression, "I know you have better-
negotiating skills than that. How else would you get a
woman to share a space with you much less sleep with
you?"

"I might've been drunk," I grunted and
shouldered my way past her. As soon as I edged into a
room, I was immediately halted by a guard. A wall of a
man dressed in a dark suit put a hand on my shoulder and
glowered at me. I didn't resist the urge to pointedly roll
my eyes then raise my chin to him, even though he
probably had a good fifty pounds on me. "Son," I
grunted like it was something to be impressed about.
Well, as a prince I guess it was.

The other man's eyes narrowed further before he
took a cursory look about the broad room that had
serviced the complaints of our people for generations. It

was empty save for my father on his throne and his attendant quietly discussing something. It looked as if they hadn't noticed that I had barged in, but I knew better. "Your grace," the guard that had stopped me spoke loudly enough for his voice to carry. "Demetri Hass, Prince of Ashouvania, is here to see you."

"As if he doesn't know who his own bloody son is," I growled at the man holding me back.

"Very well, Gustov. Let him in," my father's tone was cultured, giving no doubts as to the type of education he grew up with. I imagine it was similar to my own, though probably better because I did shirk quite a bit of my responsibilities when I realized I didn't want to rule. "Demetri," he said my name like it was both a greeting and an insult. "May I ask just what your sister did to get you to return home in the event you try to run away again?" He spoke as if I was still a teenager and he had caught me sneaking out, not as if I had been gone for months.

I rolled a shoulder as I approached his throne, taking in his appearance. It was quite evident where I had inherited my looks from, it was damn near like looking in a mirror, and it gave me a good idea how I would look when I got older. Instead of dark brown hair, his had long gone gray; it looks more regal instead of old, so it left you guessing his age. I had hoped he could rule forever and save me the trouble of having to. "I'd prefer to keep that to myself," I said in a tone that was similar to his. "I'm only here to announce my return and get that lecture you so love to give out. Then I'll be happy to go to my room with no video games or television as punishment."

His eyes narrowed, and he dismissed his attendant. For the life of me I couldn't remember his name, so he could openly glare at me. "Just what were you doing gone for so long?" He paused to cup his chin, "No, wait… I would rather not know. I will let you figure out how to handle any illegitimate children that may come to call on your own."

"Assume I didn't get a vasectomy while I was gone?" I countered.

A door slammed open, and we both turned to see my mother, in a modest blue dress suit. "You did not do that," she snapped. She stalked across the marble floors to me with anger in her blue eyes, and her gray hair pulled back into a classic chignon. "If you don't give me grandchildren," she took a breath, and I could see the amount of guilt she would inflict upon me.

While my father dealt out shame, my mother was an artisan of dealing out guilt. I deflated because I couldn't handle both at the same time added with the distraction of not knowing how Meghan was. "I didn't," I admitted bleakly.

"Oh good," she seemed to deflate, too. All the rage she had approached me with melted away and she immediately launched herself at me, wrapping her arms around me in a tight hug. "Don't scare me like that! It's bad enough that I will have to wait for Nadine to decide when she will start having babies. I was counting on you to bring home a child first."

"I'm not even thirty, yet," I complained.

"I had Nadine when I was twenty-five," she sighed heavily and stepped back to straighten my coat and shirt. "It is not asking too much. Especially seeing how you brought a girl home with you."

I grimaced and spared my father a glance; he had gotten up and approached as my mother had attacked me. "A girl that we have purchased clothing for that will only survive her the week," he pointed out as if there was something to that. "Do not count on it to be something serious. After all his reputation precedes him."

"I assume nothing," she said as she smiled at me. "I just hoped for the best."

I rolled my eyes and decided that I was better off not letting the old man get to me, "She will be at dinner. You will be able to meet her there." I straightened and took a step back, "I'm betting she won't meet your requirements anyhow, even if there is nothing between us."

"You will not be leaving again," father said in a tone that brokered no argument. "It's time you realize that you have to grow up. You are far too old to be living this lifestyle."

Of course, he would say something like that.

I didn't bother to argue; I stepped away from my mother and bowed to him. "I will see you at dinner," it would take a hell of a lot for me to find a way to escape again anyway. I would explore it later when Meghan went back to the States.

I turned to leave them and found my way up to the second floor, finding the main hall that my room and my sister's occupied. I didn't know what room Meghan was in. The stress began to catch up to me, and I could only stare down the door lined hallway helplessly. I knew where my room was, that was easy. But I didn't know if Miss Janseen had done as I asked. While the stewardess of the castle generally followed orders, sometimes she had her own interpretations of how orders should be followed. So, while I said I wanted Meghan close, that could put her in the same hall but as far from my rooms as possible.

I didn't have the patience to go from room to room. Right now all I wanted was to crawl into bed beside her and listen to all the little noises she'd make in her sleep. I was tempted to call out to her and see if she would come out to me.

It was aggravating.

"Deme?"

I looked over a shoulder and saw her standing in the doorway of a bedroom that was two doors down and across the hall from mine. I groaned in relief, figuring she must have heard me coming down the hall. I didn't bother to answer; I just went to her and wrapped my arms around her. I took a deep breath, taking in her scent.

"You okay?" she asked lightly as she leaned into me.

I hummed and just stood there hanging on to her. "Yea," I heaved a sigh and pulled away. "Think I could drag you out the door and to a car without you making much of a fuss?"

She laughed a little at my expense, something I didn't care about. "You just got back home, and you're already trying to run away again," she sighed and pulled away, much to my distress. There was just something about her that was making me feel so much better, "Why run away?" She pinned me with a look as she tilted her head like she couldn't possibly understand why I would want to give up the chance to rule.

"Too much responsibility. Have we met? I am a horrible person," I started while keeping my hands on her shoulders, touching her seemed to help. "You can't really argue with that either. I don't have the sense to help people or be diplomatic when it's necessary. Putting me in a position to lead people is only doomed to failure."

She cupped my face in her cool hands, halting the tirade I had started. Her big blue eyes pulled me in, and right at that moment, there would have been nothing I could do to get away from her. Of course, I didn't want to. I was much more comfortable being pinned by her gaze.

"The fact that you're worried about the kind of leader you would be," she started, "just shows that you would be a good one. The fact that you worry about the direction that you would take your country shows it, too.

Worrying about the outcomes is important." She socked my shoulder with enough force from her little fist that I had to step back, "It means you're not as self-centered as I first thought."

"Thanks," I grimaced because I knew it wasn't a compliment. "I think," I started to edge her back into the room she had been given with the intentions of merely having a less public display of affection.

"Oh no," she pulled away and stepped out into the hallway, giving me the first chance to appreciate the slacks and blouse that the shopper had picked up for her. The pastel pink of the blouse seemed to be paired nicely with her pallor; she had managed to soak in some sun. The color looked good on her, and I was more than eager to see if the color had soaked in all over. I tugged up the silky material thinking I might get a glimpse of something more. "You don't get to distract me," she slipped out of my grip. "You can take me on a tour."

"A tour?" I tried to guess the time. A Jet-lagged mind made it harder to guess. I ended up stepping into her room to check the elaborate clock that was on the wall. "We only have a few hours before dinner," I winced. "Not something I can skip out on, no matter how much I want to," I looked back at her helplessly. "Need more than that to get a proper tour in."

"That should be enough time to give me a basic without all the bells and whistles," she gave me a jab at my side. "I've never been in a castle. You've taken advantage of me enough now it's time for me to see how a prince lives."

"It's not as glamorous as it appears," I snipped, but hooked my arm around her shoulders. "But we'll do what we can. I'm going to say you owe me one after this. No complaints about feet getting tired because you are in for a long walk."

17

Meghan

We spent two hours combing the hallways of the ancient looking castle and going over the history of it, as far as Deme knew.

"Granted," he spoke with an air of boredom that was far too obvious. "This was shit that was hammered into my head since birth."

I chose to ignore his tone. The castle was very gothic, a little too dark for my tastes but still beautiful. There were stained glass windows everywhere, which Deme told me depicted his ancestors of the past. There were two in particular dedicated to the world wars.

"We've never had much of a military. It's more of a citizen's militia if anything. But it takes a lot to live in these mountains. While we had to fold on both accounts, we were sure to give the enemies hell where we could."

History had never really been something I really took an interest in. But I listened nevertheless, completely entertained by what he was showing me as well as the baritone of his voice as he spoke.

"You grew up with all of this, and you have this rich history behind you that shows you the way," I felt the need to point it out. "What makes you think you'll fail when it's your turn to take the crown?"

He rolled a shoulder, and his expression darkened, "I have been a disappointment for a while now. Disappointing a country, even a small one, isn't something I'm keen on doing."

"Are you a good person?" I asked curious about his opinion of himself.

He grunted and shrugged, "There are worse people in the world than me. I wouldn't necessarily call myself a good person. I know my father wouldn't either."

"So," I paused for a beat to consider his answer. "You're basing your opinion of yourself on what your father thinks?" He pulled us both to a halt, mostly because I had my arm wrapped around his. "What about what you think?" He looked down at me, his expression blank and I couldn't imagine what was going through his mind at that moment. I just felt this urge to reassure him. "If you truly believe that you're a bad person and you'll make for a bad ruler then you will be. But if you know you're better than that then you will be. Don't let someone else's opinion make the judgment of the type of person you are."

"Thank you," his voice sounded hoarse. "I really appreciate it."

A door opened ahead of us garnering both our attention. The woman that had led me to the room I was staying in stepped out; she spoke with a heavy accent that took me a moment to decipher, "Prince Demetri. It is time for dinner."

"This," he turned to me, "Is where you will see what I am talking about."

It made me apprehensive, but I let him lead the way to the dining room. A massive table ran the length of it, looking as if it could have sat a hundred people. A chandelier hung above, looking like it was made up entirely of crystals with the way it twinkled. The table was sparsely set, only offering one side set for the family. A place was set at the end, and two were corresponding on both sides. I noted Nadine and a woman that had very similar facial structure as her, obviously her mother. I was taken aback by how beautiful she was. Her hair might have once been the rich dark color that was Nadine's and Deme's, but it had long gone gray. I watched her stand, her expression schooled to be welcoming. I could only imagine a number of people she had played hostess too.

"You must be Meghan," she bent forward at the waist and curtseyed. "I am Edda Hass," she straightened and stood tall. "Nadine's and Demetri's mother." She didn't mention she was also the queen. She didn't have to.

"It's a pleasure," I said, and I struggled to reproduce the curtsey she had given me. It was in no way as graceful as her. "Meghan Reed," I said just in case they didn't get my last name. The smile she gave me was dazzling like she was pleased that I introduced myself to her. "I uh…," I struggled with an explanation as to what I was. "I rented the house that you own in Miami and somehow got talked into coming home with your son."

She laughed, and I thought it was real, "Really now?" She gestured for me to sit and did that herself, "How did that happen?"

Deme pulled the chair out for me, and I couldn't hide my surprise. I looked at him like he'd grown a second head and stood there; he rolled his eyes and gestured to the chair. "I do have manners," he grumped.

I sat down, and he pressed the chair forward. "Your daughter is very persuasive," I said with a bit of a grin.

Nadine didn't even make an attempt to look embarrassed, "It is an art form."

"So you were renting the house on Amelia Island?" Edda wasn't deterred from the subject at hand, "That's how you met Demetri?"

"I might have used Aspen as a diversion in case I was being looked for," Deme interjected from beside me, settling in closer to me than the head of the table. "It was still warm, hard to resist."

"Do not worry," Nadine spoke up before her mother could voice another question. "I made sure she was refunded for having had to share a space with him. I figured that was the best way to handle it."

"Nadine," was growled from beside me.

"That's not necessary," I spoke up. "Even if he wasn't a part of my plans," I stopped myself because I could see how that would be construed. I didn't want to seem like I was hung up on him. I didn't want that thought to occur to him, not after the conversation we had before we ended up in another country. It left me grimacing and fighting the urge to look at him. His mother looked curious, and I could feel Nadine eyeing the both of us as if I had just handed them something important. I bit my lip so I wouldn't blurt out an apology to him. "It's not necessary," I said again weakly.

"Do not worry," Nadine said to me.

It didn't set me at ease. I had messed up with that, and it was evident.

The double doors that led into the dining room opened, and everyone else at the table stood immediately. I hurried to follow suit. I glanced at Deme and noted his bored expression before I glanced back at the door, he didn't seem upset. I wouldn't be asking though, at least not until we had a moment alone.

A man that could only be the King of Ashouvania strode into the room; he wore a light blue button-down with the sleeves rolled up to the elbows and a pair of slacks. He looked so casual that I was surprised, though I don't know what I expected. Maybe a crown? Jewels? He looked at all of us and scoffed loudly, "Bloody hell, sit-down. No sense in any of this right now."

"We have a guest," Edda spoke in a light tone as she sat down at his command. I got the feeling that was why everyone stood out of respect for him, but it seemed like a habit that wasn't practiced when they weren't entertaining company.

He paused and pinned me with an indifferent dark gaze. This would be what Deme would look like in the future. Mister Hass didn't look old in the least, though there were fine wrinkles on his face and he had gray hair as his wife did. "Is it just a guest or a representative from another country? I was under the impression that this was the girl he shacked up with while he was gone."

I didn't know how to take that. I sat down uneasily and looked away.

"Don't be insulting," I heard Deme hiss from beside me.

"Oh?" His father sounded as if his interest was quirked. "Are you meaning to tell me that there's something between the two of you when you have never had any interest in any other woman outside of a day?"

The rest of the party sat, and Nadine motioned with her hand, catching my attention. The other woman looked sympathetic and carefully mouthed 'It will be okay.' I guess she was probably used to her father.

"It's been a week," Deme retorted. "More than that. Even if there was nothing between us, there's no reason for you to be rude to her. You can't tell me after all the etiquette crap I had to deal with growing up that you have completely dropped everything you expect me to use."

"Oh, a little more than a week?" The sarcasm was far too obvious. "Have you proposed yet? Am I expected to offer her an allowance, too?"

"No," I snapped because this wasn't something I wanted to be a part of. "No to both of those questions." I took a breath to gather the little bit of courage that made me speak up together, "You're not responsible for anything where I'm concerned. The only consolation I expect out of any of this is a ride home since Nadine insisted that I come along." My pride hurt, I'd been through enough. I didn't want to deal with this, too. "You don't need to worry about me trying to siphon anything from you or your family. Just the reason why you don't need to refund the amount that I spent on booking your Miami home," I decided I didn't have an appetite then. I stood because if this was going to be what dinner was like I would be able to stomach it. "Thank you for this opportunity. But, if I could be afforded a ride back to the States that would be appreciated. Thank you for your hospitality, your Majesty," I bowed to the man at the front of the table.

I didn't care about etiquette or diplomacy. I was more worried about getting out of there before he could make any more implications about my character. I wasn't a whore, and I wasn't going to sit by while someone implied that I was. I didn't expect Deme to propose either.

I made it out into an unfamiliar hallway before anyone could object. I had no clue where I was or how to get back to the room I had been given. Frustration added up, and it became an effort to not cry. I started walking in favor of just standing there looking like an idiot. Of course, I was going to get lost. I made it down a hallway before I got disoriented, the first door I opened proved to be some sort of staff pantry. There were three people in there looking as if they were preparing plates for the evening dinner, they all immediately stopped and looked at me. I didn't have a clue as to who any of them were; I'd only been introduced to Miss Janseen.

"I'm lost," I said helplessly.

The three of them exchanged looks. "Dinner?" The man asked and motioned towards the plates they were setting.

I shook my head, "Bedroom?" I could only hope that they would understand. I didn't know if they spoke English at all and it would be my luck that they didn't.

"Upstairs," the man spoke with a thick accent. He paused and spoke to the two women, I assume instructing them to finish. Then he came to me, stepping out into the hallway. He took my hand and led me towards a staircase I didn't see before. "Upstairs," he said again.

I nodded my understanding and bowed slightly, awkwardly, "Thank you." He returned my nod and left me there, going back to the work of serving the royal family dinner. I made the trek upstairs alone, relieved that I finally found the way only to have that relief vanish when I got to the top of the stairs. Aside from the stairwells, there was nothing else other than doors that would lead into bedrooms.

The only consolation was I knew my borrowed room was close to the stairs. I took the time to search each of the rooms that looked as if they could be the one I claimed, but I knew as soon as I didn't see my things that they weren't. Of course, the last one to be checked was mine, and I was so tired I didn't even care how long it took me to find it or the fact that I was hungry. I went into the classically decorated room to the large canopy bed and fell onto the plush mattress. One thing I would miss was the soft, comfortable beds I've slept in. My bed at home didn't compare in the least.

I stretched out and considered undressing for bed before I decided to just concentrate on relaxing. This was probably my only night in the castle. I could only imagine how my exit was considered a slight upon the crown here. I figured should pack, and there were a few things I should do before the inevitable flight home. However, I couldn't force myself up to do any of it; the last day had been too much.

As I was wallowing in self-pity, there was a knock at my door. I forced myself to sit up with a groan. I didn't want to get up further, "Yes?"

"Open the door," Deme's shouted from the other side. "My hands are full."

I didn't try to hide my groan as I got up and jerked the door open ready to give him a piece of mind. Only, I saw him standing there with a tray of food looking just as irritated as I felt.

"Sorry," he huffed and breezed past me and took the tray to the little dinette set that was set by the massive fireplace that sat opposite of the bed. "I just figured you might be hungry," he then flopped down in one chair like he was entitled to it.

He wasn't wrong. I was hungry. But I didn't know what to make of his appearance. "Am I in trouble?" I figured that might have something to do with his visit.

The expression on Deme's face changed immediately, and he stood, "No. He was out of line." He closed the distance between us in a few steps, "He was making jabs me for some of my poor choices. Him insulting you was uncalled for. You," his hands cupped my shoulders, and he bent so that we were at eye level. "Aren't like what he thinks, you are far better than he could imagine." His voice lowered, "Are you okay?"

There was something about having him so close and being reminded just what had been implied about right in front of me that seemed to shake me. I wasn't going to crack. I wasn't going to let the words of an angry old man get to me.

"I will be. When will I be going home?" I imagined the flight to New York would be a whole lot shorter.

Deme straightened and cleared his throat as he seemed to prepare himself for whatever bit of bad news he was about to drop on me. He opened his mouth then stopped seeming to change his mind, "Do you have a really big bag you might be able to smuggle me into?"

I wasn't expecting that. All I could do was stare at him.

"So, that's a no?" He heaved a sigh, "Honestly, one of the reasons I came up here was because I had hoped I could talk you into staying. I thought I'd ask that just in case I could get lucky." He tugged me towards the dinette sat and motioned for me to sit, "I can't force you to stay, but I can make a bigger ass out of myself by begging you to stay."

I sat at the table to see what food he had brought me. The plate had various cuts of meat that looked to be either chicken or turkey, and there was a vegetable that I was unfamiliar with. I carefully tasted it before I forged ahead with eating.

"Why would you beg me to stay?" I watched him carefully.

"Because," he looked uncomfortable. "I didn't know how much I would enjoy you being here until you got here. You make it easier being here. You make it easier dealing with him," he looked at me, and I saw the seriousness there. This wasn't a line he was feeding me, he was being real. There was nothing flirtatious about this. I could see the fear in his eyes, he was afraid of what I might say. "Say you'll stay." He didn't hide anything with those words.

I put down the fork and swallowed hard, it was more than just to get rid of the food I was eating. I needed to get past that lump that had suddenly formed in my throat. "I'll stay," I managed to say without croaking. This was trouble looking back at me; this was going to make it so much more difficult to leave when it was time.

He got up and took a step towards me, offered me a hand. I took it, and he pulled me to my feet. From there, he came down to me. He kissed me sweetly, not as if he were striving to stoke a fire within me. I felt emotions building that I couldn't control. I leaned forward against him to return that kiss, hoping with everything in me that I wasn't doing something stupid.

The sweet kiss immediately became heated, as if he had been holding back his want from me since the conversation back at the house in Miami. Of course, he hadn't. Every time I met his gaze I could see how he felt. He didn't make any effort in hiding it. I had tried to get some space from him and it all that space was boiled over as he kisses turned hungry.

I gave in because everything he felt and wanted was reflected back to me and I was consumed by it. My arms went up and around his neck, drawing myself closer. The taste of his lips and the feel of his tongue as it eased its way past my lips was enough to make me forget the ordeal. His hands didn't wander; he didn't take the opportunity I was giving him, despite the growing heat from his kisses.

He pulled away, gasping for breath, "I didn't come in here to do this."

I started to pull away, struggling to cover my own heavy breath, "Why did you come in here?"

"Well," he still stayed close, and I could drown in his dark eyes. "First to apologize for my father being an ass, second to make sure you didn't go to bed hungry."

I decided I wasn't going to leave, with a confidence I hadn't felt before I arched up on my tiptoes. "I'm hungry," I breathed as I leaned in close to him. The only thing I could do was hope he didn't confuse my meaning.

From the expression on his face, he knew what I meant. He looked like he might question me, his brows drew together, and I was afraid of what he might say. So, I took the initiative that I didn't think I was capable of. I caught his mouth with mine and kissed him in a way I was sure would get my point across. He didn't pull away, or attempt take control from me. His hands drifted, sweeping down my back one moving lower to cup my ass and pull me against him. I felt his erection against my thigh and any doubts about this burned away. I wanted this, and I wanted him. Even if it was only for a little while longer.

"To the bed," he instructed when he managed between kisses. We moved together, me going backward and him guiding so that I didn't stumble. As soon as my hips hit the mattress, I began to tug on clothing, mine or his, it didn't matter. There was too much between us. He followed in a fevered suit; his button-down was up and over his head between a hurried breath. Buttons went flying as my blouse didn't seem to want to cooperate, I didn't care. As soon as my chest was exposed he dropped to his knees before me so fast that I was left dizzy. It was then I realized the difference in our height was ridiculous, but I wasn't about to complain when he trailed up my stomach from my bellybutton to just below my breasts. He shoved my bra out of the way, fidgeting with it from behind but not bothering to wait for it to open; he just latched onto the first breast that he uncovered. His tongue and teeth left a wake of goose bumps across my chest and stomach, it was like he was a live wire that I had dumbly grabbed hold of.

"God," he groaned as he mouthed his way from one breast to the other. "I missed these," he latched on and sucked hard until my toes curled. "Your breasts are delicious, and I don't think I can go that long again." He curled his hand around the back of my neck and tugged me down into a hungry kiss.

The slacks I wore were shoved down, and his tongue traced a track back down my stomach, sweeping along the waistband of my panties. I held my breath, my eyes fluttering closed as it became obvious just what where he intended to go from there. He snagged my panties with his teeth and started to tug them down, as soon as they were down far enough they were forgotten just above my knees as he seemed to be more interested in nuzzling my mound and licking my thighs.

My legs trembled; I wouldn't be able to stay standing for this. Just the knowledge of what he wanted made it hard to stand. Deme was a man that seemed to have no problem diving between my legs and feasting on me until I begged for mercy. The memory of the last time he was there throbbed to the forefront of my mind, and I couldn't help but drag my fingers through his hair. I wanted this just as much as I wanted his cock in me.

"Get on the bed," he voiced a hoarse commanded that I readily followed. I crawled back onto the bed, but when I got too far, he tugged me forward until my ass hung off the edge. My panties were tugged the rest of the way off and thrown over a shoulder, followed by my legs right before he dove in.

My breath caught in my throat at the feel of his mouth on me. He licked his way along the length of my sex until he found the hood over my clit to suckle on. I couldn't help the way my thighs twitched and tightened around his ears, the feeling was too intense that I couldn't just lay there. My hips rolled up towards his mouth because I definitely didn't want to discourage the assault he was making on me. He went on to press two fingers into me, roughly fucking me with his hand.

"This is turning from a want into a need, love," his voice cracked through the haze of pleasure I was drowning in. "Stay here," he demanded as my hips rocked against his hand. "Stay with me."

"I will," I keened arching into his hands.

He stood, shifting between my thighs and hovering over me all the while his hand kept working me. "You're going to stay!" His eyes were alight, and I couldn't tell if it was just with lust or something else.

I was too overcome to know for sure. His fingers curled upwards, and all I could do was moan and cling to the bed sheets. It was all too much, I was going to explode. I heard the rustle of what I took to be clothing, the jingle of a belt and I felt him hot against me when he finally pulled his hand from me. I could only quiver, clenching muscles that were throbbing and so close to completion.

Then he said the world's worse words, "Fuck." It came out like a curse that cut through the fog. He was over me, and his cock was resting against my lower stomach, his expression was pained, "I didn't bring any fucking condoms with me."

That was enough to get everything back to me, I still throbbed. If he left me like I was right this second, it would be painful to both of us. I wouldn't be satisfied pleasuring myself.

"Where are they?" I asked.

"Back in the states," his pained look only seemed to deepen. "I could get someone to run out to the shops, but that could take hours." There was a look of defeat as he lay down against me and I felt the full weight of him as he seemed to just be content with lying naked against me.

It wasn't enough for me. There was one way to do this, but it was taking a massive chance. I ached. I wouldn't be able to go to sleep like this and I knew he wouldn't either. I took a breath, hoping I wasn't going to end up regretting this later. "Don't get me pregnant," I whispered in his ear.

He tensed on me, and he shifted so he could look at me, his brows were drawn down. "What?"

"Don't," I shifted and hooked my thighs around his hips, feeling his hardness against my opening. "Get me pregnant." I hoped he'd get it as I started to carefully thrust myself against his length; it was just short of him sliding into me. I clenched, this wouldn't be enough. "I want you in me," I breathed I couldn't wait.

I felt him shudder, "Are you sure?"

I could only nod, but that seemed to be more than enough of a response for him. He pulled away just enough so he could adjust his aim. He gave me one final chance to change my mind, rubbing the head of his cock against my opening teasingly.

"Last chance, no take backs," his voice was low.

And men had the audacity to call women teases. I huffed out my growing frustration and lifted my legs up so that I could curl my hands around my knees. I tried to press forward so that the head of his cock would press into me.

"Stop playing," I couldn't help but whine I was so keyed up. He had done this to me, "Fuck me please."

"Oh," he gave me a grin. "You said the magic word, I guess I have to now," he took hold of one foot, seeming all too pleased with the fact that I had spread myself for him, and slowly pressed forward.

A groan rattled through both of us as he slid into me, it felt that good. I arched back into the bed, trying to resist the urge to rush him. He had put me on the edge of cumming, and I was still so close. Once he was fully sheathed in me, he pressed me further up on the bed, crawling with me so that we stayed connected. "This," he gritted as we moved, "was a horrible idea." He began to thrust, leaning into my legs for support. "Shouldn't have done this."

"What?" I managed, but I knew as he built momentum I wouldn't be able to say much else. I'm surprised I had the wherewithal to question him. What he said seemed to be important, but with each hard thrust into me, I lost track.

"Didn't mean to say that out loud," he laughed a little shakily. He kept moving though, he sounded just as breathless as I felt. At this angle he was in so deep I had forgotten what he had said, all I could do was hold on and rock with each thrust. "Not going to be able to pull out in time," he gritted between clenched teeth. "I can tell you that already."

That should have bothered me, but in the heat of things, it didn't. He pulled at my legs until I released them, the angle changed and the depth that he reached was lost, but he pressed against me in exchange for it. He distracted me with kisses, and I clung to him as each thrust pressed me closer and closer to oblivion. I'd never wanted something so much before. With the way he pressed against me, each thrust had his pelvis rub into my clit, and I could only moan against his mouth. I could only cling to him harder in hopes that I wouldn't fall to pieces when I finally came. He road it out, burying his face against my neck and increased his pace. If his pained grunts were any indication, he wasn't far off himself.

He caged me in, holding himself up on his forearms, not that I would have been able to go anywhere. But it made me feel like we were closer with his brow pressed to mind. He leaned up and stilled, "Not yet." He jerked out of me I thought he was finished up until he flipped me. I made a noise of protest until I felt him slam right back into me. I gasped out as he began to thrust into me hard.

I didn't have anything to hold onto now. With each hard thrust, I was thrown forward, and I had to find purchase in the blankets, so I wasn't smothered by them. The new angle had him going in deeper, and he brushed against things in me that had me crying out with just how good it felt. I was amazed by just how quickly he was edging me to another orgasm. It went so quickly all I could do was hang on.

I barely had the chance to catch my breath from the first one, and here he was forcing me through another. The first had left me in nearly a puddle; the intensity of the sensations he was giving me now made me realize this one would be so much more.

I didn't even attempt any sort of restraint. There wouldn't have been a chance. It rocked through me in the same rhythm of his cock, pounding out with a force that left me seeing stars. It was hard to breathe, I could only gasp. It was too much that all I could do was quiver and whimper. It was just too good.

I felt heat erupt in me and a string of curses came out from behind me in a spert. Deme jerked out of me again then I felt the heat of his cum against my ass and the back of my thighs.

"Fuck," he gasped out and then I felt his hand press against my lower back forcing my hips down. I stayed on my stomach, not bothering to move even with my feet hanging over the side. It didn't matter, I was much too comfortable.

Deme pressed into my side, "As soon as I can feel my legs I will clean you up. Promise." I could only imagine how he felt. I couldn't fault him as I was a pleasant, numb puddle. A shower could be had later.

There was no point trying to fight the exhaustion. I had come in here with the intent of sleeping anyway. There seemed to be an added bonus of having Deme at my back. I went out with little effort.

18

Demetri

If there was anything that could take away the stress of being back in this dungeon, it was having Meghan here with me. That was obvious before we had sex. It was much more obvious now that she let me have her again. I wasn't going to be too much of an ass and expect to be able to go in raw every time I managed to get her going just enough to not care about protection. I made sure one my attendants went into town for condoms. The knowledge of having one less thing to worry about, coupled with the knowledge that she had agreed to stay, practically had me humming.

"Demetri," my mother called down the hall. Of course, having Meghan couldn't take away from the fact just where I was. "Can you join your father and I in his study?"

"Bugger," I grumbled to myself because it was like I was still a bloody child.

This could either be because I hadn't been joining them for meals, or because father was miffed that I was in the castle without being available for him to berate. I followed her down the familiar path of hallways to the ornate door that led to his office or study. Honestly, I didn't know the difference. I swore when we entered room that it seemed to have a problem making up its mind as to where or not it was a library or a place where a decorator decided to dump wood tones and plaids as if we were Scots. My father sat behind an obnoxiously large desk that was stained a dark color so that he stood out like a flame behind it with his gray hair. Or was it starting to go white now?

"What do you want?" I used as a greeting. There was no point in beating around the bush. I flopped into one of the stiff plaid wingback chairs that were positioned in front of his desk.

I saw him bristle at my nonchalance. I didn't bother to straighten, but I did resist the urge to throw a foot up onto his desk.

"How long is your friend going to be staying?"

At least he didn't sound insulting as he spoke about her. That was a relief that I wasn't ready to show to him. The question had caught me off guard though. Mostly, because I didn't have an answer. In the heat of the moment, she agreed to stay, but I doubt that would survive me forever. Though if I could keep throwing it until we were both delirious, there was a chance I might get lucky with having her stay a bit longer. Since I didn't have an answer, I decided to deflect. "Why?"

"Your mother implied that the relationship you have with this girl may be serious," he cleared his throat, and he seemed to be making an effort to avoid my gaze. I looked from him to my mother, brows rising. Were they watching me that closely?

"Nadine mentioned there was some attraction," I watched my mother fidget under my gaze. "I mean more so than what we have seen with other women. And Gregory mentioned you had him purchase you some condoms from town," she flushed and had the grace to look embarrassed. Maybe this had something to do with that crack I made about having a vasectomy. "I needed to know. If you are serious, you have my full support."

"She's a common girl," my father paused to tap at a laptop he had opened. "Her education only went as far as a Junior College, and she's spent two years as a paralegal with no attempts to seek better employment," he glanced at me. "Or any sort of advancement. She only speaks English."

"What are you trying to say?" I growled out.

"You could do better," he finally looked at me fully. "I have offered princess after princess to you, and many had taken an interest in you. I am sure your advancing age will not affect that at all. Must you be attracted to someone so unworthy?"

"Alard," my mother sounded offended for me.

"Being blunt," he responded, and I watched him look at her as if she might give him support. Instead, she just folded her arms and stood at the corner of his desk. "The person he weds will be who helps him lead this country. In all likelihood, she is more concerned about getting a hold of crown and money, nothing more."

"Stop," I sat up and leaned forward. "You haven't even spoken to her. All you did was insult her and look up her history," I started without thinking. "Have you ever thought that a common girl might have the best concepts behind doing what's important? Like connecting with the people of her country and having the right kind of outside mindset? If I were to marry a princess, it would be just about money and being eye candy." I thought back to that night I had taken Meghan to the club, "Meghan's more than that."

"And you know this after a week?" He looked at me like he thought I had lost my mind. "How can you have any sort of judgment to her character? How long did it take for you to get into bed with her?"

I stood, glaring at him now. "Give me some credit," I gave him a smirk as I bowed mockingly. "Doesn't take me long to get into the pants of anyone. You should ask a few princesses you threw at me," then I went to the door. I'd had enough. "Instead of demanding gifts or anything else once we arrived she questioned why I left in the first place. Why wouldn't I want to be the prince of a country and take advantage of everything I had? My path was set for me, and I didn't have to struggle. What hardships would I know? I'm pampered." I waited for a beat at the door. "After she met you she stopped asking," it felt good to let that tidbit out. I opened the door and stalked out. I was done with my father.

19

Meghan

Well. I can see that Nadine isn't just persuasive, but she's stubborn too. Despite my protests, the money that was supposed to be used to forget James was back into my account. I didn't know what to make of it. Should I be grateful?

I didn't want to take advantage of these people. I could imagine the type of women that Deme saw before me, and even if they just thought he was wealthy, that would still probably seek extravagant gifts. Them forcing this money back onto me, plus the wardrobe, seemed a bit too much. I could only imagine how much all of it cost. Maybe I should try to pay them back? There wasn't a single tag on any garment, and I had no way of calculating anything. It was beginning to get frustrating.

There was a tap on the door, and I didn't get a chance to respond before it opened. I looked up from my phone to see Deme lingering in the doorway. "Can we get out of here?"

I slid off of the bed and frowned at him, "You're not wanting to run away again, are you?"

He smirked a little bit and rolled a shoulder, "If I thought I could get away I would snatch you up, and we would be gone." He heaved a sigh and repeated his question, "You want to get out of here?"

"What did you have in mind?" I was curious, he looked just about as frustrated as I felt, but it didn't look like it would involve him trying to get frisky.

"I promised you a proper tour, didn't I? Grab a coat, and we can head to town," he nodded as if he liked the idea and turned. "I will get my own and a driver. Give me a minute."

I couldn't hide my excitement after he left the room. I had been more than eager to get out of the castle after meeting his father. It was way too obvious that I wasn't wanted here and while I avoided it all by staying in the room I was borrowing, I felt cooped up. How I was going to get home? I didn't know. Though I no longer found myself caring about James and whether or not he was still in our apartment. I didn't care about whether or not I could afford it on my own. All I knew was what I had with Deme was on borrowed time.

I had my coat, and I turned out the lights of the room before going to wait out in the hallway. I was half tempted to go find Deme. But I knew I'd sooner get lost than I would find him. So I waited patiently since he made it sound like he would only be a minute for him to grab a coat. I took a second to look at the weather and grimaced. *Thirty-one degrees. Maybe I should get a scarf, too?*

"Meghan?" I turned to see Nadine approaching.

"Nadine," I gave her a clumsy curtsey. "I didn't know you were still here."

"I stay through Christmas," she informed me. "After that, I go back to being a dutiful wife," she didn't hide her expression at the idea. It made me wonder about the marriage she had. I assumed it was arranged. Did Deme have something similar setup?

I had a sinking feeling in my stomach at the thought. But I knew I had no rights to him. There wasn't much I could do if he had a fiancée but feel bad for the girl. Did that make me the other woman? I clutched at the front of the blouse that I wore, crumpling ruffles and wrinkling the flawless linen.

"What are you doing out here?" Nadine prodded. "Were you planning on going somewhere?"

"Deme had promised to take me on a tour," I started numbly.

I heard her chuckle, and I looked at her. "The only other person that I have ever heard call him Deme is me," she sighed lightly. "You have replaced me it seems," she didn't look upset. "Just to make sure this isn't a ploy of his to sneak off with you, I think I shall tag along. That okay with you?"

"I don't mind," I tried to smile at her, but I could feel it fail miserably. "Can I ask you a question?"

"Of course," she came in closer as if she thought I was going to share a secret with her. "What is it?" she asked in a lowered voice.

"He's not," I swallowed hard. "Promised to anyone, is he?" I had never considered the fact that he might be, even after finding out he was a prince. I might have been able to survive finding out he was after the stint we had in Miami, but now I didn't think I would be able to manage it.

She snorted out a laugh, and I didn't know what to make of it. "Oh," she waved a hand as if it was a joke I couldn't get. "Our parents have tried to secure him to countless women. Princesses and politician's daughters left and right all his life. Demetri does not just have a pension for running away, but he has a horrible pension of breaking hearts." She gave me a smile, "He is not attached to anyone. I promise." I released a breath and the sick feeling I had before seemed to seep away, "Oh, but the fact that he is a heartbreaker is not something that has you put off?"

I fanned myself with a hand, "I think I've already figured that part out. Before you found us in Miami, I was trying to figure out just what he was playing at, and I couldn't get a straight answer from him." I released a sigh as I thought back on it, "He is far too attentive for someone that is just interested in sex."

"He's being attentive?" She looked curious.

"It felt like he was trying to romance me," I couldn't help but shrug at her. "It was more than I expected," I nervously ran my fingers through my hair. "I guess I shouldn't look into it too much. I'll be going home soon. Um... I forgot to mention that I'll need a flight home."

She gave me a nod and a smile, "You had a flight from Miami international to JFK for the third. I have already arranged with our pilot a flight to JFK from here on the same day."

"Thank you," the relief I felt was almost overwhelming. "How much is the cost of--"

"Do not even," she snapped her fingers at me. "I am well aware that I did not give you much choice to come home with us. You are an unfortunate casualty of circumstance. I figured if I could get you to come along that Demetri would agree without much fuss. And I was right," she said smugly. "That is saying something."

"What is?" I asked.

"Nadine," Deme barked out from the staircase close by. His expression was hard. Had he heard our conversation? I thought quickly trying to figure out what could have angered him.

"I was going to tag along," she smiled at him. "I have some business in town. You do not mind, do you?"

"Afraid I will make for another escape?" Deme shot back.

"Actually, I can explain away talking your girlfriend into joining us here," she moved past him and headed to the stairs. "But I think doing it a second time just might qualify as kidnapping."

I laughed uneasily because I couldn't really disagree with her there.

Deme quietly led the way downstairs and to the front doors. The conversation was halted, mostly because I preferred to be careful when it came to the stairs. I didn't like the idea of tumbling down them, and if I wasn't careful, I would find a way. As we approached the large doors in the foyer, I was familiar with everyone starting to suit up for the colder weather. I stopped thinking about paying them back for the thick pea coat that had been bought for me. Instead, I bundled into it and was grateful.

The limousine was smaller than the one that had taken us to the airport. We had to squeeze in the back seat, and I was placed between them. I gathered from the small vehicle he had planned for it to just be the two of us. Another hint at him trying to romance me. I just wished I was in a position I could look out the windows instead of separating the animosity that seemed to be rolling off of Deme toward his sister.

"What did you need from town?" I tried to delve into small talk. To see if she would admit to needing anything or if she just decided to tag along for the sake of it.

"I was hoping to pick up some last minute things," she smiled at me. "The man I married does not celebrate Christmas, the main reason for me being here. But, that does not mean I cannot supply him with a gift. I was so distracted," she paused to give her sibling a look. "That I had completely forgotten to get him anything. So, I thought I would take advantage of your adventure. I hope you do not mind."

That was an idea. "How is the shopping in Ashouvania?"

"Stabak," she supplied. "That is the name of the capital city. While it does not rival Paris or New York in fashion by any means, we have the benefit of a wealth of craftsmen in our country. You can find many beautiful things that are handmade that will be one of a kind and easily an heirloom."

I hummed at that, "What's the primary language that your country speaks?"

"Dutch," she supplied. "I am sorry, but you will probably want to stay close. I am doubtful that you will find many in town that speak English. Not to say it is not possible. Just," she shrugged helplessly. "Father had both of us study abroad. He wanted us to master as many languages as possible."

I knew they were both educated and it was obvious that English wasn't their first language from their accents. I really didn't measure up. I looked away as I considered her words. I was in their home, and it would be likely that I would stick out like a sore thumb. And the fact that they were both royalty was impossible to ignore. I was used to dealing with rich clients on the occasion that they accidentally found their way to the office that I worked in. Mister Marks, one of the attorneys I worked for was in a good position himself.

But where was I at? I was wondering how I would afford the tiny apartment I lived in and wondering where I would go from here. The money that had been refunded would definitely hold me off for a little bit to pay bills, but it didn't necessarily mean I would be able to finish the lease with it. It made me rethink what I was doing here.

This couldn't be more than a fling. Regardless as to whether or not he intended to romance me, I couldn't let it grow into more. I couldn't give him my heart, and I couldn't let him get attached.

It hadn't been obvious before, but it was so obvious now. I couldn't play at being something I wasn't, and I doubted that I would be someone that could stand by his side. I could never be a princess. I didn't have it in me to help rule a country. That wasn't me. I didn't have the education for it.

I glanced over at Deme and saw his brooding expression reflected in the window. I couldn't let him invest too much, which seemed to be exactly what he was doing. I decided then the best way to handle this particular trip was to soak in what I could and not let my situation upset me.

The car rolled to a stop outside a store lined block, they looked quaint and were decorated for Christmas with holly wreaths and small trees in the windows. A small crowd was going along the sidewalk paying extra attention to the window displays. The weather was brisk, but that didn't seem to stop anyone. Not even Nadine or Deme seemed to be bothered by it. While I wasn't originally from New York, I should be used to the cold after living there for so long. But I still felt like I was missing a cap, scarf, and maybe even gloves would have been nice.

I bundled up tightly as I strolled beside Nadine, looking in each window with open curiosity. I'd lost track of Deme, but I figured he wouldn't have just left us here. I did notice that the driver had followed us. There had also been a second man in the front seat, whom I assumed must have followed Deme. I grimaced because it was easy to figure out. They were bodyguards. It made sense now.

"He was supposed to be taking me on a tour," I glanced over a shoulder. "But he disappeared."

"He did not expect me to want to come," she hooked her arm through mine. "I imagine he had some plans that I have dutifully ruined," she gave me a grin then rolled her shoulders as if it weren't a big deal. "Honestly I had only come because mother asked me to. Plus I needed to get Abir something just for the sake of it." She pulled us up to a halt and seemed to spot something in a window, "Let's go in this one and see what they have for sale."

I couldn't' decipher what the sign said, but I followed her in and noticed what it really was. It looked almost like a jewelry store. There were other things, and the more I browsed it was obvious that everything was handmade. Nadine immediately left me to pursue a display case, and I took the time to look elsewhere. There was an elaborate plaque the looked as if the designs were burned into the wood. There was a script on it, too, but it wasn't something I could read. Not that it mattered as it was still beautiful. There was a similar series with intricate designs framing a small paragraph on stained wood. Then I noticed the delicate looking ornaments also cut from wood, they looked gorgeous.

I wish I knew what they said.

I went to the display cases that Nadine was at. Inside was handcrafted jewelry all of which looked lovely. There were beaded things that looked to be carved from wood that did nothing but jump out of the case at me. Designs were etched into their surfaces, and I was amazed that they looked so beautiful. I glanced further down, and I noticed a difference in what was present, they were also handcrafted but without the wood theme. There were necklaces and bracelets with metal plates, words were printed on them and while I couldn't recognize what they said I knew the trend. They were all so pretty and feminine, even in a language I couldn't read. That was until I saw a bracelet with a thicker chain.

I hummed as I considered it, "Did you find something you like?" Nadine appeared beside me, apparently done with her shopping. She looked at the case and seemed to fight to see what had gotten my interest. "Did you want me to get the clerk's attention for you?"

"Actually," I pointed towards the bracelet I was considering. "Do you think a man would appreciate that?"

"A man?" she looked at me then down at what I was pointing at. "Or do you mean my brother?"

I couldn't keep but flushing, "You know what I mean."

She gave me a smile that lit up her entire face, "I think it would not matter what it was. The fact that you thought of him to give him a gift would be enough." She waved at the clerk that was busy with another customer and turned back to me, "Did you just want the bracelet? Meneer Kranz also does engraving if you like."

I paused for a beat. What would I want it to say? Then it seemed completely obvious. "Yea," I looked to her. "I can think of something to put on it."

20

Demetri

I have never wanted to do my sister more bodily harm than I did today. This was supposed to be a moment, and while it didn't take a whole lot of effort to plan it out, it was frustrating to have her ruin it for me. I didn't know what I was thinking. Honestly, I envisioned walking hand in hand with Meghan as we looked at the shops. Maybe picked up a gift or two for her. Something shiny, maybe something to convince her that she didn't really need to go back to the states. Or maybe just something to get her to stay just a little bit longer.

I had the misfortune of coming up on the conversation that involved her return. I wasn't expecting it to pierce me like it did. The attachment I had on her only seemed to worsen. Now, knowing I only had days left, just added to it.

It wasn't as if I could have snatched her and run away, though it was definitely a thought. The way I had managed to slip away last time had been more along the lines of luck and a bodyguard that was a little too relaxed and familiar with me. He was a great mate; it was a pity that he was no longer employed by the family. I hadn't thought to look him up since I got back, but it would be something I would have to do. I owed him.

The man that was tailing me now seemed far too intent. He watched me like a hawk. If I sped up in an attempt to lose him, he was quick enough to catch up. I had ducked into a clothing shop thinking I was in the clear only to have him pop up behind me with a smirk and a: "Your majesty."

I gave up after that and just got used to the hulking man following me. I had shopping to do. I didn't consider purchasing her more clothes; we had a personal shopper that was better when it came to judging style than I was. When I saw a jewelry store, I decided to go with the original plan.

As soon as I stepped in the door my shadow starting getting a little too mouthy for my tastes. "You are going to buy her something from here?"

How did he know who I was shopping for? I gave him a glare. "It's imperative for the growth of our economy that we put money back into the nation. I would rather buy from a shop run by my people than order something from another country." That should have been obvious.

"But you are okay with getting a commoner from another country?" he asked, his tone holding disdain that I wasn't prepared for. "You think that part is okay?"

The gut reaction I had was to snap at him, but something stepped in and held me back. Was he speaking his own thoughts or those of my father? "A woman from another country," I spoke idly instead, not taking his bait. "Is less likely to be a relative."

He snorted in amusement, and I proceeded to ignore him. His opinion wasn't important. I didn't care if anyone saw her for what she was. Their opinions weren't important. I just put more effort into looking for the right thing. It wasn't until I moved down to the rings that I saw the right piece. The stone stood out among the others, even though it was a modest piece.

"If you get her that," the man behind me spoke up again. "It will be assumed that you are proposing."

"That will be between her and me," I said hotly, refusing to look at him. It was decided though, and I wouldn't be talked out of it. I flagged down the clerk and hoped that I could guess her size.

21

Meghan

I was more afraid of dinner with his family, again, than I wanted to admit. When Deme pulled out my chair for me, I nearly stumbled when I moved to sit down on it. The table was set with a festive theme, and I felt horribly underdressed when I saw how well put together Nadine and his mother were. I repressed any sort of distress though; given that I didn't have anything other than the small wardrobe I was given. I had no cocktail dresses or anything for a party. There didn't appear to be any guests, so the only people I could offend were those present.

Deme was dressed just as casually as I. I don't know if it was because I didn't have appropriate attire and he knew it, or if this was his usual style. Maybe I was reading far too much into it. It was becoming a nasty habit, my overreaching. That was probably how I got into trouble with James in the first place.

I shook that off and made a quiet vow to myself about not allowing myself to envision things that weren't there.

Borrowed time, Meghan, remember? There's no sense getting attached to a handsome man when you will be leaving in a few days.

Deme's father came out with a flourish as he did the first night I had arrived. When we started to stand out of respect, he barked out not to. This was a hard man to understand. I got the feeling that he was used to commanding a room, even as a leader of a small country.

"Miss Reed," he said coolly as he sat down. "How kind of you to join us," he seemed to be purposely ignoring Deme, who was seated to his right. "I trust you have enjoyed your visit to our home?"

I hadn't seen a lot of it, out of fear of getting lost in the maze of hallways and rooms I had restricted myself to the room I had been given. So, aside from the trip to the shops and the short tour Deme had given me I hadn't seen anything.

"What I have seen of it," I started. "Your country is very lovely." It seemed like the best answer I could offer.

He hummed lightly as the first course was served. They were little savory cream pastries that I didn't have a name to, I waited to see how Nadine was eating them before I followed suit. I knew my manners weren't going to be as refined as the rest of the tables so I did my best to seem as if I knew what I was doing while covertly watching the woman across from me. I think I managed alright; I didn't get any sort of reprimand from anyone. Though I doubted that would have happened. No one was even paying attention to me and how I ate each course that was set in front of me. I had no names for the food that was presented to me, nothing looked familiar. But I was determined to try everything, and after the first bite, I definitely wasn't disappointed.

"How long do you intend to stay?" Deme's father started up the conversation again midway through the second course.

I had to pause, replacing the spoon into the shallow bowl. I tried to consider my words carefully; I hadn't spoken about my leaving to anyone save Nadine. I cleared my throat, "I'm scheduled to return to work on the fourth. My flight from Miami was due to leave on the third. I thought it was best to keep the same schedule."

"So," his mother spoke up, there was something about her expression that looked pained. "You won't be staying long?"

I didn't know how to take that. I glanced carefully at Deme, his expression was blank, and he continued eating as if there wasn't a conversation going on around him. I gave his mother a tight smile, "Unfortunately not." I didn't know what else to say.

His father nodded, seeming to relax and accept my answer at face value. It wasn't until near the end of the fourth course that he spoke again, "Did you have any intentions with my son at all?"

I was carefully cutting through meat that I thought was beef, but had a succulent sweet flavor to it as it seemed to melt on my tongue. When he asked the question, I felt like I had been put on the spot. How do you answer a question like that? I carefully put down the knife and fork, trying to formulate an answer. I don't know how long I sat there, but I felt a warm hand fall on my knee and give it a light squeeze.

"I didn't," I admitted at first. "I didn't have any intentions with your son," I only hoped I didn't offend him while I spoke. "When I asked him a similar question he didn't have an answer for me then," I couldn't help but shrug helplessly because it felt like I was forced into a spotlight. "I don't intend to push for something that isn't there. Nor do I assume to take advantage of his position as a prince."

I watched as the king sat back into his chair at the head of the table, his dark eyes narrowed and piercing through me. I could see judgment there; it was much too obvious that he didn't think I was worthy. "And you will not go to any of the gossip rags in your country to sing the song of your failed romance?"

"That's enough," Demetri growled from beside me.

I cleared my throat and forged ahead despite the monarch's picking. "I don't," I answered honestly. "This was a private thing between Deme," I paused for just a beat to correct myself. "Demetri and I. I would have preferred that it stayed that way after my vacation was over regardless if we were here or if we were still in Miami. Sharing it with anyone else would just keep it from being the good memory I prefer to treasure it as."

"She is a lady," Edda commented lightly, seeming to be just as irritated by her husband's line of questioning as her son. "Your assumptions are offensive."

"With Americans, you can never tell," he said as if it were nothing. "Anything for the glorious five minutes of fame," he went on eating his meal like he wasn't insulting me.

"When I first got here I wondered why he would run away," I said without thinking. "I thought he was just irresponsible and I couldn't imagine why anyone would run from being a prince with an easy life planned out for them with money for whatever they wished," I paused to take a sip of wine because I had started and now I was going finish it. "But, this is only the second time I've spoken with you. You're combative and insulting to a stranger. How do you treat your son? How early was it that you started doling out this verbal abuse?" I met his hardened gaze with a sudden courage I didn't recognize but sitting here it all made sense now.

The dinner table was silent and I didn't look away from Alard to see the reactions of everyone else. My temper had gotten the better of me, and instead of doing the smart thing, like walk away, I had let my mouth run off without a thought. The insult seemed to be taken seriously, or he didn't have a retort. I didn't know which though I had a fear that he might call for a guard to take me their dungeon. I paused for a moment at that thought. I didn't know if this castle had a dungeon and I quietly wished I had kept my mouth shut when Deme spoke up.

"I was thirteen," his voice was so soft I didn't hear him at first. But it was enough to draw my attention to him. His expression was a blank mask, and it looked as if he were just speaking of the weather or if he were commenting on dinner. "Thirteen," he verified with a nod like he had gone back to check the date.

My mouth went dry, and everything seemed to make sense all at once. "So," I turned a glare to his father, "You're surprised when he ran away? Did you treat Nadine the same way?"

"He did not," she offered from the other side of the table, looking sullen.

"She was the favorite," Deme murmured from beside me.

"That's enough of this insolence," he growled back.

"It is," Edda interrupted her husband. "You have done enough," I was surprised when I heard it, and I looked to see if it was directed at me. Instead, I saw her glaring at her husband as I had been. "You are chasing away a woman he clearly cares for simply because you have deemed her unworthy," that revelation didn't surprise me. "It is Christmas," Edda's voice rose a little. "I have both my children under one roof after months of worrying whether or not my son would come home at all. If you cannot address your son with respect, then you need not address him at all."

"And how do you expect him to lead this country without my help?" His tone sounded begrudging. "You expect him to do this on his own?"

"He could," I started, and I looked at Deme with a smile. Edda caught my gaze as I finished my thought, "But I will see to it that he has help."

It felt like things were slipping into place and I felt relieved when we left the table. There was still tension in the air, but the conversation had been forced, even with Nadine's charm. Deme led me to my room and gave me a polite kiss good night.

"I need to think," he said quietly. "You don't mind if I leave you here for the night, do you?"

Honestly, I couldn't blame him. "I'm sorry I ruined Christmas for you," I winced because I expected that there would have been a whole lot less tension had I not been there. Things would have probably been a whole lot less stressful if I had just stayed in the states.

"You didn't ruin it," he stepped away from me. "Honestly, that's about on par with every Christmas I can remember."

That hurt to hear. "Things will get better," I said to him, even though I had no way of knowing for sure.

"They already have," I got a wink for my troubles before I watched him go down the hallway. He was two doors down from me and across the hall. I knew he wanted to be alone, so I was going to let him be. But I decided to file away which door belonged to him for later.

I went into my own room and began to prepare for bed. I was already dressed in a tank top and shorts when I realized I had forgotten to give Deme his gift. Now didn't seem like the time to go slink into his bed, after all, he had asked to be alone, and I doubted it had been an hour since we had parted ways. I was carefully turning down the fire, amazed with the fact that even with as old as the castle appeared to be it still managed some modern conveniences. I hadn't bothered playing with my phone, aside from sending check-ins to let Jodie know I was still alive, so I wasn't aware if there was Wi-Fi that would stretch out the length of the imposing property. I could only imagine what my bill was going to look like when I finally got home, so I refrained from using it more than a spare text here and there.

A knock on my door brought my attention away from the free time I had on my hands, and I stood to answer it, not paying attention to my state of dress. I was surprised to see Nadine at my door, though I guess I shouldn't have been. She gave me one look and flushed, "I did not pay any attention to the hour. Forgive me. Could we talk for a moment?"

"Sure," I stepped away from the door so she could come in. I wasn't sure what to make of this.

Nadine came in but didn't bother to sit. "Today was horribly uncomfortable, and I am terribly sorry for that. When I came to get Demetri, it was because my mother was so sure he would not come home on his own. When I found you there I thought it would make life easier on him," she took a breath and fidgeted with an embellishment that was on her dress. It was one of the few moments she didn't have an air of confidence about her. She looked unsure in front of me. "Father is very critical; he expected the best from both of us. I did not realize that he had been so hard on Deme until it was pointed out. And you are right when you expect the worse of someone for so long they bend to your perception," her face twisted a little. "I had been so hard on him every time he turned down a prospect of a bride. I thought he was doing it just to make father angry. After I was betrothed to Abir, I had thought he was making light of his duty. I did not get to pick who I wanted to marry. Why should he have that same choice?"

"Do you not love your husband?" Curiosity got the better of me, and I couldn't help, but ask.

She rolled her eyes as if I was missing the point, "Abir is a good man, and yes, I have grown to love him." She took a deep breath, "It has become apparent that I have been unfair to my brother. I have been exceptionally hard on him. And looking back on some of his poor choices I can see what influenced them."

"You can help him," I pointed out. "I don't think he holds it against you."

"Deme has always been caring, even when he was whoring around he was never callused about it," she admitted with a sigh. "You have been good for my brother," she pinned me with a look. "What can I do to get you to stay?"

That caught me off guard, I couldn't think of a logical reason for her to ask me this. "If I stayed how would that help?"

"You would help him go down the right path and be a better person," she pointed out. "You have already started him on the right path. If you stay here, I can only imagine how much he would grow as a leader and a person."

There was something about the prospect of giving up everything that frightened me. While I liked Deme and I knew he felt the same, I wasn't sure I was ready to give up everything to stay in a new country. "I can't," I winced. "You have to understand what you're asking of me," I started immediately when I saw her stricken expression. "You're asking me to give up friends and family. I like Deme, I do," I paused to catch my breath. "But is that love? Being able to support him and hope for the best for him? There's more to love than just that."

"And if we offered you a salary for it?" She folded her arms over her chest, and it was apparent with the way she schooled her features that she was determined to get her way again. "We could put you on retainer. Name your price; you could have your own home off of the castle grounds."

"Why are you asking me this?" I tangled my fingers in my hair as I tried to keep from sounding panicked.

"Because I love my brother," she snapped at me. "Despite all the hell I have given him growing up, I love him, and I want what is best for him. You are a good woman; you can set him on the right path."

I shook my head, "Your father would disagree. This has been a fairytale experience, but I have to get back to the real world." Her defeated look gave me hope that she was going to give up on getting her way. "You want your brother to be on the right path then you can take the steps to make sure he is."

Nadine started to wring her hands, her brows drawn down as she considered my words, "You are right, of course." She stopped fidgeting to give me a level look, "In that respect, it would probably be for the best that we do not entertain this any longer." I blinked trying to figure out what she was saying before I could ask she had her phone out and was tapping away at it, "I will arrange a flight home for you in the morning. I am sorry, Meghan. But I need you to leave as soon as possible."

My chest felt hollow like my heart had fallen into my stomach. "If you think that's necessary," I couldn't argue with her. It felt reminiscent of when I was corralled out of the house in Miami. "I'll need to pack my things and get to bed if that's how it's going to be."

Nadine nodded going to my door, she kept up her work on her phone as she jerked open the door. She paused, not looking at me, "I am sorry. It was nice meeting you, Meghan. I wish you the best and safe travels."

I couldn't do anything but bend to what she wanted. If I protested, it could be taken the wrong way. So, I nodded and tried not to let the closing door hurt me too much. The first thought I had was to pack, but the only clothing I had that belong to me was already in my bag. I would leave everything that didn't belong to me. I went to make sure I had my toiletries put together, and it took me maybe thirty minutes to ensure that I had an appropriate outfit for the weather, something I had packed with the return to New York in mind. I was tired, and I started to climb into bed with the intentions of getting much-needed rest until I saw the box that held Deme's gift.

I couldn't leave without making sure he got it. I grabbed the box, and without much more than a thought, I went out my door and down the hallway to his.

22

Demetri

I had to have space to think and having Meghan close by only made that seem impossible. Of course, dinner didn't go as planned, nothing ever went as planned where my father was concerned. And of course, a sore spot got dug into, something I didn't like to think about. There was nothing entertaining about being second and the fact that I grew up with the knowledge that I was good for nothing only seemed to reinforce the fears in my mind.

I couldn't sleep, I didn't bother trying. I found a bottle of bourbon I stashed in my closet for just such an occasion and cracked it open. I lost track of time after that, staring in the fire of my personal hearth and wondering where life would go from here.

When someone knocked on my door, it only seemed to insight me with a burning anger that I only could contribute to my father. "What?" I snapped, not bothering to get up. I was well past any care for being polite. If Nadine thought she was going to come in here and try to be a peacekeeper I wasn't going to give her the time of day.

But, instead of Nadine, it was Meghan that opened my door. She came in without any further instruction, setting down a little-wrapped case onto my dresser. She had a pair of shorts on that put her legs on full display and a thin tank that did nothing to hide the curves of her breasts. The burning anger I felt quickly turned into something else entirely. She had my full attention.

Meghan didn't say a word as she came to me. Instead, she leaned down over me and kissed me. I couldn't keep from groaning into her mouth when I got a taste of her sweetness. It seemed to pair just right with the bourbon I had been drinking. How did she know I needed her just then?

I started to wind my free hand into her hair, wanting her close to me, but she didn't seem to be having that. Much to my delight, she knelt between my spread knees instead. She propped herself up on the edge of the seat as she began to work open my belt and slacks, it gave me a glorious view of her breasts until she worked my cock free. I hadn't gotten fully invested in the idea of bedding her tonight, but it didn't take long for the gentle caress of her hand to make her case.

Her lips were quick to follow the progress of her stroking hand, taking me from half-mast to a dull throb as soon as her lips closed around the tip of my cock. My fingers went nerveless, and I dropped the tumbler I had been drinking out of before. I didn't bother trying to contain the groan that she pulled from me with the swipes of her tongue and the suction she applied as she started to swallow more of me.

"Meghan," her name came out in a gasp as her cool fingers worked into my slacks to cup my balls. I couldn't help but relax back in the seat as she bobbed her head along my length. I needed to see it and to touch her, I shoved her hair out of her face, and I watched as she pressed further down, so she had the majority of my cock down her throat. I groaned as she constricted around me with a swallow.

All my thoughts were forgotten in favor of this vision she gave me of my cock disappearing past her lips. That was until she was intent on swallowing every inch of me. She held that position, choking on my cock until I saw stars. When she came up for air, I couldn't only gasp, "You're gonna make me cum if you do that again."

"Do you want me to stop?" She asked before going back to sucking on me.

"Oh no," I couldn't keep my eyes from closing at the delicious feeling. "But now I want to fuck you, too. I'd need a breather to get hard again so that I could do that."

She hummed, and I couldn't help but groan as it vibrated through me. I wasn't going to last long as she kept working me in her mouth and with her hands.

"Stop," I managed before she swallowed much more of me. She pinned me with those big blues while she still had her lips wrapped around me. Her tongue was doing things to me that made it an effort to think of anything else. "No, stop," I gritted because it felt too good. "Come here so I can fuck you properly."

She finally let go of me, though she used her hand to stroke my cock until I couldn't help but thrust up into her fist. My hips had a mind of their own, and they didn't seem to care about what I wanted.

"Are you sure?" She purred back.

"Fuck yes," I growled at her and tugged her up into my lap. Before she could protest, I caught her mouth hungrily, not at all bothered by the flavor of her tongue against mine. All I cared about was the fact that there was too much clothing between us. I had far too much to drink to worry about decorum. I tried to force her shorts and panties down so that they were out of the way, but at some point, they refused to move, so I tugged until the fabric gave. The rip didn't seem to give her pause, nor to the fact that protection should be a necessity. I should care, too, but I was far too gone to care. As soon as I felt the damp heat of her pussy against me, I took aim and thrust up into her sweet hold.

It was too good, I couldn't think past thrusting up into her raw and just how much I needed it to be like this. I felt every inch of her, and the only thing I could think I wanted more was those tits in my face as she rode me. I tugged her tank top down until it became another casualty of her late night visit. It didn't matter, none of the ripped clothing mattered in favor of what was happening right now. Clothing could be replaced, this moment couldn't.

Her moans rang in my ears like music, and I made sure that every noise she made would be punctuated by me leaving a mark on her. I dug my teeth into her collar, and I sucked a little trail of marks between her breasts all the while she bounced on my cock; little marks that would make her mine. I felt her start to quake around me, and all I could do is hold on. Her bouncing ride stopped, and I started rocking up with a force that only seemed to set her off more.

She cried out, her fingers digging into my shoulders even through my shirt. It looked like her clothing wasn't going to be the only bits that were damaged. I could feel the dampness of my slacks on my thighs. Had she gotten that wet from sucking me off? Oh, that thought just added fuel to my fire. I wasn't going to be satisfied with just one go, even if I couldn't drag this first one out to be longer.

It didn't occur to me to pull out when the throb became too much. It didn't even bother me to erupt inside her, thoughts like that could be saved in the morning when I wasn't ball deep in her. All that mattered right now was that she was still wrapped around me and I could touch her, taste her all that I wanted. I didn't give a damn about consequences right now.

"You're staying," I panted against her neck wishing I could make her stay. Wishing I didn't have to worry about her impending departure that was coming up far too quickly. "Right here until I can get up enough for round two."

Round two was a definite thing, and if I could manage it, I might try for round three.

She laughed and then distracted me with kisses and wandering hands. The last thought I remember having was how I was going to get her to the bed. I could manage that without pulling out. All the while she had been here I hadn't fucked her in my bed yet. I wanted to go to sleep with the scent of sex on my sheets. I wanted the smell of her in my bed. That was something I was going to make happen. I was going to make sure it did.

After a little breather.

23

Demetri

When the light finally cut through my closed eyes, I rolled over, not ready to wake up and start the day. The only thing that kept me from dropping back off was the fact that I was alone. I squinted to see if maybe she had just scooted out of my grasp, but no. I was in my bed alone. That was enough to wake me up. I sat up and tried rubbing the sleep from my eyes.

Had I dreamed it? I squinted against the persistent sunshine to see my room empty. There was no sign of Meghan had even been here, except for the fact that I was naked in my bed. I leaned down and the scent of last night's activities was pretty pungent. The bed wasn't damp, so it wasn't a wet dream. I got up; my clothes were strewn about in a trail from the dinette to my bed. So that was a good sign that someone had either stripped me or my dream wasn't a dream. There was a glass tumbler by one chair, and there was a heaviness to my head that seemed to support the fact I'd been drinking.

"Meghan?" I called out, just in case she was in the en-suite bathroom. I waited a beat, and when I didn't get an answer, I looked in. The lights were off, the room was empty.

What the hell?

Irritated, I got a pair of sweats on and made my way out of my room. I went down the hall to the room she was staying in, I didn't bother knocking. She had some explaining to do after leaving me alone after a night like that. I threw the door open only to find the room empty. The bed was made. It was like she was never here.

I stalked into the room and threw open the closet. Her clothes were there, or at least the ones the shopper bought for her were. They were neatly hung on the rack as if they were never worn.

"What the fuck?" I couldn't help bout of anger I had in me. I blindly fisted the fabric in the closet and jerked it out of the closet, flinging it across the room without a care to where it landed.

"What on earth are you doing?" I looked up to see Nadine in the doorway, surprise evidently that I was destroying a guest room.

I don't know what came over me, but the only thing I could think at that moment was that somehow she was responsible. "What the fuck did you do?"

"I am not the one destroying a guest room, you are," she looked at me like I had lost my mind. "How are you going to ask me what I did?"

"Where is Meghan?" I asked, maybe I needed to clarify for her. Maybe she couldn't see the very real stress I felt at this moment. The very real fear I felt eating me alive.

When I didn't get an answer from my sister, I took a step forward, because of course, she had something to do with this. Why else would Meghan leave out of nowhere? Why would she leave ahead of schedule?

"What the fuck did you do?" I might have yelled, from the way she flinched I could see that she was finally on the same page as I was.

"She wasn't going to stay, Deme," her calling me that pet name, the same name that Meghan had called me from the start didn't do anything for the fevered rage I felt right now. "She wasn't going to stay and help you get into the position you need to be in to take the crown. If she was not going to be willing to stay for you, why should she still be here?"

"Because I wanted her to be here," I snapped at her. I started to stalk forward towards her, able to envision my hands wrapping around her neck. "Why couldn't you just leave it be?"

She smartly backed away, and I had to stop myself. Nadine was no longer the princess of Ashouvania, and while I wasn't familiar with her husband, I was sure he would probably miss her not returning home.

"And how would this be any different from her leaving in a few days? How would that be better?" Nadine shot back, trying to reason with me.

"I would have had more time with her," I retorted. "I would have been able to make an effort to win her over to the idea of staying with me." I had to reel myself in before I did something I would regret before I got myself in bigger trouble than I was in right now. "How long has she been gone?"

"I got her up at five," she murmured lowly. "And put her on the plane at seven. She's been gone for three hours."

I didn't have any idea what time it was. But three hours, I could work with that. I pushed past my sister and started down the hallway. I could catch her.

"She was going to New York?" I more asked myself than Nadine. I wasn't thinking past the fact that I wasn't ready for her to be gone. I wasn't ready to go without Meghan. I wasn't done with her.

It was like I had a need for her that I couldn't wrap my mind around. I needed her that was all I knew. I was determined to make sure I had her back. Even if that meant leaving right this second to find her back in the states.

I made it halfway to my room before Nadine spoke up, "She took the jet, Demetri." At least she was smart enough to not use that pet name again. "You'll have to get to the airport and purchase a ticket to the states. You will probably have to make connecting flights.

That is if there is a seat available the day after a major holiday."

"Fuck off," I hollered over my shoulder. "You did this, you think of a way to get me to New York now."

"No." That stopped me in my tracks; I had to clench my hands into fists to stay where I was at. The desire to wring her neck was so strong right now that I didn't know what kept me from doing it. "You are not going anywhere," she stated firmly. "You are going to do what you can take your place as crown prince and prove to father that you are capable of being a proper leader."

"Fuck him and fuck the crown," I growled out, I kept it low wanting it to be something I kept to myself. I was angry, I was hurt. I didn't know that I entirely meant my words, right now my only thoughts were on a plane flying home.

"What even makes you think you can talk Meghan into coming back with you?" Nadine prodded. I turned to glare at her. "When I first met her it looked as if the two of you were having a spat. Why would she come back? She has a life to get back to. If you want her to come back what do you have to offer her?"

That made me stop. It was like I was crashing right back into reality. What did I have to offer her? "A crown? A country?" I said out loud, that would be enough. Wouldn't it?

"If Meghan was that type of woman she would have never left," Nadine had closed the distance between us. She looked mournful as if she felt bad for sending Meghan away. "She would not use you or your Royal status. If you want someone like Meghan to stay with you, to come back home with you… you have to offer her more than that."

I felt the adrenaline from my fit leaving me. The night before, that glorious night she gave me before she left, started to catch up with me. I was angry still, seething. But, the beyond the rage I felt… I was tapped.

"What would I need to offer her?" I looked at my sister trying to see if she would give me this.

For a minute, I thought she was going to leave me wondering in the hallway, torn to try to figure out just what she was getting at. "There's one thing everyone wants, Deme," her voice was soft. "If you want Meghan to come back and be with you then you need to love her."

I didn't have a response to that. What was I supposed to say to that?

Nadine didn't bother to give me any more insight. Instead, she left me to go into her own room. I heard her engage the latch. Good. That meant I scared her. That shouldn't have made me feel better, but it did. It wasn't much comfort once I got back into my empty room. I felt directionless, and I had no way of figuring out a solution to this.

Did Meghan tell Nadine she wanted me to love her? Do I? I honestly didn't know. I knew that I enjoyed her smell. I adored the feel of her soft body against mine. I slept best with an arm around her middle, a hand cupping her breasts and my nose buried in her hair.

Now I didn't even have that.

I leaned back against my door and tried to figure out a way to get everything I wanted back where it belonged. I slid down the old wood until my butt hit the parquet flooring. I was content to sit there, I didn't want to get back in bed and disturb the smell of her there. The chair we had started it in would probably smell like us, too. But, aside from her lingering scent, there wasn't much I would have to remember her by. The idea made my chest burn as if someone had taken a hot coal from the fireplace and pressed it against my skin.

Her scent would fade. It would go out with the wash and then what would I have left?

I looked up, drowning now in the thoughts of how much I would miss her. Something caught my eye. She had put something there when she first came into the room. I reached up and snagged the neatly wrapped box off the table. She left me a gift, and I never got the chance to give her mine; I had been far too distracted by her. I took the time to unwrap the simple festive paper before I pulled the cardboard box from it. I popped off the lid and took note of a bracelet. The chain had thick links in it and was attached to a plain plate. No, I turned it over. There was a simple message engraved into it.

'Prove him wrong.'

24

Meghan

Despite being on a private jet with all the amenities, I was still jet-lagged to the point that I felt zombified when I disembarked from the luxurious ride. I was led to the private airport where there was a cab waiting for me. I guess that was the end of Nadine's favors. I was going to have to pay for my own ride home.

There was a mild temptation to call Jodie, but that might have been asking too much from her. Instead, I shot her a text to let her know I was back in the states and was hopping in a cab to get home. Hopefully, the traffic wouldn't take too long. I climbed in the back and gave the address to my apartment and tried my best to stay awake.

It had been a bad idea to go into Deme's room last night. It was a doubly bad idea to do that without any sort of protection. It wasn't too late to stop at a clinic for a plan B pill. I could do that after I managed some rest. I wasn't in any hurry. I knew even with his questionable behavior before I met him that he was clean. And while I was on the pill, something I hadn't thought to stop even after I caught James with another woman, I would still make sure I covered all my bases.

I could only imagine what his father would say if I ended up pregnant. I pinched the bridge of my nose. It hadn't been a horrible vacation all and all. If I hadn't gotten attached to him in Miami, I would probably be okay right now. It wouldn't have hurt as much as it did to leave. But, I couldn't stay there. Not with the animosity I could feel coming from his father. Even if Nadine had worked out a salary for me, given me some sort of off the wall title that would make it look like I deserved it. It would have still been wrong. I doubted I would be able to be with Deme in any kind of professional sense. What would that make me? A concubine? A mistress?

No thanks.

The best thing I could do, for the both of us, was to come home. It was earlier than expected, but it was the eventual outcome either way. I would get over this. Not that it was the same kind of ordeal I had been facing with James. Instead of dealing with a betrayal I was facing something different: a romance that wasn't meant to be. I wouldn't look back on it with regret, I decided. It would be a fond memory I would have. That was a better way to look back at it.

The ride to my apartment was long and cost more than I would have liked to pay. But considering most of my vacation had been refunded back to me, I wasn't going to complain. I was so tired that I was just happy about the prospect of finally being home.

It was a shame I had completely forgotten about James. Not really, but I wasn't expecting him to be here when I walked in the door. He was seated on the couch, looking as if he hadn't bathed yet with plastic wrappers surrounding him. He held a console remote in his hand, and it became clear he had spent the majority of my trip on the couch playing video games.

Now he was staring dumbly at me like he hadn't expected me to come back.

"Why are you still here?" I asked.

He blinked, seeming to grasp that I was in fact there and stood, dropping the game controller. "I've been trying to get a hold of you since you left! You can't expect me to leave without getting the chance to plead my case here, Megs," his nickname for me didn't even affect me. I had blocked his number because I didn't want to hear from him either.

"James," I said slowly as if I were talking to a child. "There's no case to plead. I caught you in bed with another woman," I went back to the bedroom deciding that I would rather not deal with him and I would much rather just be at home. "You have had over a week to get your stuff and get out. That would have been the adult thing to do. The considerate thing to do."

"C'mon, baby," he followed because of course, he would. "It was one mistake." I doubted it. "You can't hold this against me. We just signed the lease on this place."

"I signed the lease on this place," I corrected him. "Your name is only on the utilities. All you have to do is pay off this month's utilities, and then you can have them turned off."

Why was he putting up a fight? The apartment was tiny and way overpriced. I still had to hop on the train for work. Really, I probably should have looked in Jersey like Jodie first suggested.

"And how are you going to afford this place on your own then?" His tone was mocking. "Kicking me out now over one trip up is pretty ridiculous. We had plans, baby," he stood in the doorway while I put my suitcase in the corner. I didn't feel like unpacking right now. "We can still keep those plans."

"Plans change," I said darkly, glaring at him. "My plans no longer involve you. If you're not out before I got back to work, then I can get another eviction notice."

He frowned at me now, "How are you going to evict me if my name isn't on the lease?"

"Well if you want to play that game," I folded my arms over my chest as I looked at him. "I can say that you're a squatter. Everyone at the office knows that I went on vacation and I have receipts as evidence. The only thing you have that's evidence that you live here is your name is on the utility bills. Now you can either get out on your own, or you can be forced out," there was something in me that made me feel powerful. I wasn't desperate for a man's attention. I didn't need a man in my life. I had a good one, for a brief moment. Even if he didn't love me, he showed me how I should be treated by a man. And James just didn't add up where he should. "Which way do you want it to be?"

"I don't get a second chance?" He looked surprised like he thought he could worm his way into getting me to forgive him. Was he out of his mind?

Was I that much of a doormat that he thought I would let go of this? Not anymore. "No," I growled and if looks could kill I would have murder in my eyes right now. I wasn't backing down. I wasn't giving in. "You don't love me. There's no point and you being here," I said with a snarky tone. "The fact that you're trying to 'plead your case' at all just tells me that the girl you were sleeping around with didn't realize you were with someone and probably refused to take you in."

"How do you know I don't love you? Haven't I told you enough? "He didn't even twitch at the last part.

"Cheating on me makes it pretty obvious," I sat on the bed and pulled off my tennis shoes.

"You know what," he snorted. "Fine. I'll go. But you gave me until you got back from vacation. You're back early. I'll be out in a week." He pulled his phone from his pocket, "I can't believe I spent this much time with you if all you're going to do is chase me off after one mistake."

"More than one mistake," I supplied. "But that's neither here nor there. If you're going to be staying here, you can sleep on the couch. It looked like you already had set up camp there anyway."

I got a sneer for my troubles, and he turned to walk out of the room. I heard him call someone and the complaints began. Honestly, I didn't care. I got up and closed the door, then twisted the lock. I flopped back into my bed, the sheets were twisted from it being unmade, and they stank of James' cologne. The mattress didn't have the right support, and I knew as I shifted around trying to find a comfortable spot that once I woke up, I was going to be sore.

It was a harsh reality. A wake-up call I didn't want to answer. Nothing was going to be as good as it was with Deme. I was going to be stuck back as Cinderella. Even with as charming as he was Deme just wasn't meant to be my prince.

25

Demetri

I lasted a week. And I was only able to last a week because Nadine was there to deter me from doing anything. It was frustrating to the point that when she finally went back to her prince in the country she now called home, I was happy. I wasn't going to miss her. Not the way I missed Meghan.

It became clear enough that what I felt for Meghan was more than I was capable of putting into words. There was nothing that dulled the raw feeling; no matter how much alcohol I would drink in my room. Once I tapped my stash, I was forced to pilfer what was in the kitchen. That only went so long before it was noticed then reported.

"Are you developing a drinking problem?" I looked up from the floor at the blurry figure of my father. Of course, I would only go so long before he would come raining down a flurry of my mistakes back at me.

"I don't find it to be a problem," I took a sip from the bottle of brandy I had found in the pantry. It burned, and I had to squint to keep my eyes from watering.

He stepped into my room without invitation and looked down at me, "Of course you don't. What, may I ask, is the reason for this?" I considered giving him an answer, but after the way Meghan had talked to him last, I imagine he didn't care for her. And why would he? She had a connection with me, and obviously, he had a deep-seated hatred for me. I decided the only way to answer him was to shrug, let him read between the lines. "It's that girl, isn't it?"

I only offered him another shrug; I really didn't want to talk about Meghan with him. But I found my hand going to the bracelet I wore on my left wrist. There was something about it, not just its message, that touched me. It left me feeling hollow and the only way I had found so far too numb the feeling was drinking until I could sleep. Not exactly responsible, not doing as she suggested I was capable. But, I was coping. Soon I would get over the loss of her, and I would be able to get adjusted. I hoped.

"Stop drinking out of the damned bottle," he said as he walked over to the dinette. It was something I had treated like a little bar. I had a couple of tumblers and a long gone dry decanter on it. I watched as he picked up the two glasses and came back to me. He sat beside me, with a grunt, and took the bottle from me. I watched as he poured two fingers into each glass then set the bottle aside. "You can be sad and drink, but you are a prince. You don't drink out of a bottle like a homeless person."

"I thought I would save someone the trouble of having to clean up after me," I picked up the glass closest to me.

"So," he took a sip. "Why are you hung up on this girl?"

Despite my better judgment, my better judgment was drunk after all, I showed him the bracelet on my wrist. He raised an eyebrow before looking at it. When he read the words, I could see some sort of realization hit.

"Him being me? She was telling you to prove me wrong?"

I could only nod, my throat felt too tight to speak.

"Well," he sounded impressed as he let go of my wrist. "I guess she deserves more credit than I was willing to give her." That should surprise me that he was admitting that. "I will say that I am surprised she left. I expected her to try to milk whatever relationship you had for as long as you allowed her to," he paused to take another drink.

"If you think the worse of people, sometimes they feel the need to prove you right," I said lightly as I gestured to myself.

"She was right about that," he said after a beat. "There's nothing I can say or do to make up for your childhood. There's nothing I can say or do to make up for how I have mistreated you," his voice was low. "I wish I had an excuse for it. I don't."

"I wish I could say it made me into a better man," I snorted into my glass before I drained the remainder of it. "But it didn't," I took the time to splash a more liberal serving into my glass.

"I failed you as a father," he said as if I hadn't spoken. "I doted on Nadine so much," he released a breath. "I was an only child. I didn't have any siblings, and my father pushed me to be the best I could be. Failure was not an option for me."

I listened, not sure where he was going with this, before responding with snark, "I am a failure. Does that make you one, too?"

"You are not a failure," he growled at me. "While I won't argue that I am, you are not. You excelled at every challenge I threw at you. You graduated at the top of your class. The only thing I could not get you to do was settle on a woman after throwing so many at you." He paused then seeming to consider something before he went to top off his own glass, "How many of them did you sleep with before you passed them off?"

"The majority," I answered honestly because he had his opinion of me and there was no point in try to change it. "Any of them that were of Middle Eastern descent I was sure to tread carefully with. I didn't want to be the reason that some poor girl got stoned to death because I had a problem keeping it in my pants." I shrugged because they didn't matter then and they certainly didn't matter now.

He snorted, and when I looked at him, he looked impressed. That wasn't the expression I expected. I guess he didn't take advantage of the opportunities he had before he was wed to mother.

"Why are you still here?" my father slowly asked.

"I have to prove you wrong," I motioned to my bracelet like it had the obvious answer. "Can't do that if I run away again, now, can I?"

For the first time, I can remember he gave me a real smile. There was no sarcasm or anger in his voice, "Well if you need a woman to help you in proving me wrong you should go get her." He drained his glass then set it down on the carpet beside me, "I doubt that one will come back on her own. You will probably have to talk her into it. She seems to have a stubborn streak and can be mouthy."

"What?" I was confused as I watched him get up to his feet. I couldn't make sense of what he was saying. "What?" the first one didn't feel like it was enough.

"Your American girl. If you intend to prove me wrong," he paused to stretch then grimaced as things started to pop. A hazard of age. "You need to go get her. You are going to need help to do that."

"You are telling me to get Meghan?" I needed to verify. The whole conversation seemed like a hallucination. I put my tumbler down and stared up at my father as if he was actually a figment of my imagination. I was in a drunken stupor. None of this could be real. None of it made sense, the conversation or having a drink with him.

"Yes," he snapped at last seeming to lose the last bit of his patience at my asking. "And if you must wed her you have my begrudged blessing." He offered me his hand, "I have had a week of silent treatment from your mother that is more than I want to bear. Enough is enough, boy. If you drink yourself into your deathbed, then I will be to blame. That is something I won't have. I won't have your mother hating me for that."

I took his hand, and I let him pull me to my feet. I wavered so I held onto him just to be sure I wouldn't stumble.

"I wasn't drinking because of you." Though I guess I could see why he would think that after everything that Meghan had pointed out, it was easy to see why I would drink.

"I know," he squeezed my hand and gave my shoulder a pat. I was glad he understood. "But I am giving you a reason to stop drinking. Sober up and I will make sure the jet and pilot are ready."

26

Demetri

It took some footwork and hounding the financial advisor to get Meghan's address.

"This is unethical on so many levels," Grant barked before he finally caved.

I didn't care. Damn ethics. All I cared about was that everything that had been wrong with this week was about to be corrected. Getting back to Meghan was all that mattered to me. After that I was on the jet and bouncing with energy, I couldn't stay seated. I couldn't relax, not now that I knew where she was. I had her address, an apartment on First Avenue. I couldn't get there fast enough.

I had a car waiting for me, and I didn't bother with the back seat. I wanted to see where we were going as if I had any sense of directions when it came to New York. I gave him her address, "Damn the laws. Get me there as fast as you can without getting me killed."

He gave me a grin like I had issued him a challenge, "I get pulled over you're paying for it."

That wasn't something I could argue with. But as soon as he stepped on the gas pedal I immediately regretted asking him to go fast. This was a man that had the capability to wheedle his way through traffic no matter how big the car he was driving. It was terrifying.

Even then it seemed to take too long.

"I can't help traffic, buddy," the driver shrugged at me when we first got locked in bumper to bumper. "It's the nature of the beast. This is New York," he shrugged helplessly at me. Though his sympathy seemed genuine, I couldn't really hold it against him. My drive to see her again had blinded me to the obstacles that would crop up in our way. Now I wished I had been able to calm my excitement.

After about an hour of traffic, I was finally striving to find her door. When I finally found what I thought was hers I knocked on it with an enthusiasm that startled the owner. The little old woman barely spoke a lick of English, but she was able to give me directions to where I needed to go, a floor up in a building with no elevator. All of this wasn't even a clue to the life that Meghan led before we had met.

Finally, finally I knocked on the right door, and a bloody man answered.

Who the hell is this? Did she come home just to replace me? She doesn't seem the type to move that quickly.

He didn't look surprised to see me or disturbed, just offered a light: "Can I help you?"

"Is Meghan Reed here?" I quietly hoped that I had the wrong apartment, that the language barrier between the little old lady and I had been too broad. That after a week she hadn't found another man that she would prefer over me.

Instead of doing the polite thing and asking me to wait, the man in front of me just turned around and hollered in an irritated tone, "Meghan." He treated it as if it was a chore. It grated me immediately, and I couldn't help the flash of jealousy that tore through me.

I heard an answering question, her voice through the distance between us made it difficult to understand what she said. Did she come home to this horse's ass instead of staying with me?

"Someone's at the door asking for you!" he answered back to what I didn't hear her say.

The hollering back and forth started to make my head pound. The lack of sleep and binge drinking was finally catching up; I had no more politeness for the man in front of me. When he turned back to me to eye me with curiosity, I couldn't help but glower in response. I could take this man, I decided, with little effort. He looked heavier than I, but from what I could judge, it wasn't muscle that he was packing. I could drag him out into the hall and teach him how to respect a woman. How to respect the woman I wanted.

"Deme," her voice cut through my haze of anger and jealousy, and it was all immediately forgotten.

I was so caught up in my possible replacement that I hadn't seen her approach. Meghan stood there in a pair of ratty jeans and a shirt that displayed a band I was unfamiliar with. Her eyes though, they spoke volumes to me. They were wide with surprise, and there was no anger in them at the sight of me. She elbowed her way around the man that had lingered close to the door, and she stepped out into the hallway.

"What are you doing here?" She shot a look over her shoulder at the voyeur that still intended to watch despite the looks he was given. I clenched my hands into fists; he could easily be taken care of. "Please tell me you didn't run away again."

"It's a new year," I cleared my throat and gave her my undivided attention. "And someone told me I should make an effort to prove the doubts of others wrong. Are you still going to doubt me after saying that?"

I watched her lips twitch, but she bit back the smile. "I don't doubt you," she admitted and seemed to draw in closer to me and lowered her voice. "But I worry. Worry is different," she paused and finally decided to close the door, so we had some sense of privacy now.

I felt relief flood me, if she was closing the door on him, then he wasn't important. She hadn't offered him an explanation, and I was sure, as long as this worked, I would be able to get one from her later. She hadn't replaced me, yet. There were more important things to get right now. Right now having her in front of me was far more important.

"What are you doing here?" she repeated.

"You left me your gift," I pulled up the sleeve of my coat to show the bracelet that I wore. It was something I hadn't taken off since I found it. "You left an impression on me and I felt it so strongly after you left," my voice felt thick, and I couldn't contain the emotion I felt. It was futile to try. "It was as if you left and took a bit of me with you and I don't know how I'm going to survive without it."

"I'm sorry," her voice sounded small. I don't know what she was apologizing for.

I shook my head and pulled out the little box from my pocket. "You gave me your gift," I present it to her. "But I never got the opportunity to give you yours," I could see shock looking back at me, her eyes near the size of saucers. "I intended for it to only something beautiful, something that you would look at and think of me." I got down to a knee. "I need it to be more," I held the box up to her. "I need you; I need your help and your strength." I waited and hoped that she wouldn't mention the man behind her in the apartment. While the impression was that he wasn't important, I couldn't count on that. I held my breath as I waited for her to react.

"Deme," it came out in a rushed breath, and she seemed almost afraid to touch the box I presented to her. "Don't ask me this just because you're scared--"

"I'm not," I cut her off. Because that wasn't the response I wanted from her. "I am terrified, the future is uncertain. I know who I want beside me while I face it," I sounded so sure of myself. I don't even know where the words came from, but they felt so right to say. "Meghan," her name was like a prayer. I put as much reverence into it as I felt. "I love you," three words I never thought I would say to anyone came pouring out of me. "Come home with me, stay with me. You are the only person to show that you believe in me." I wasn't afraid to beg. It was an effort to not throw myself at her and beg her to take the box. "Please."

She took the box, but I didn't relax. I watched her open it, and her eyes widen in disbelief. "This is unreal," she said at last. "I can't believe this."

It hurt to hear.

I stood, shakily. She hadn't said yes. She hadn't agreed just yet. But she hadn't said no either.

"Believe it," I looked at the oval diamond, and I questioned the sanity I had to buy that when I did. "Believe it and please… stay with me." I was almost to the point of desperation, standing in this tiny hallway of doors waiting for a verdict that would decide my future.

She laughed a little, "I never had a chance to say no. Did I?" She released a breath and looked up to me, eyes shining as she leaned up to press a chaste kiss against my lips. It was like everything was finally falling into place. "I didn't keep my promise before," she paused to kiss me again, and I knew everything would be okay from here. "But I will this time, Deme. I will stay."

www.ingramcontent.com/pod-product-compliance
Lightning Source LLC
Chambersburg PA
CBHW021054130626
46552CB00005B/2091